"I told you to remove your clothes, *azizty*."

Kavian's mouth was so close then. Amaya could feel his breath against her lips, particularly when he said the unfamiliar word she was terribly afraid was some kind of endearment. She was more afraid that she *wanted* it to be an endearment, that she was starting down that slippery slope. She could taste him if she only tipped forward—and she would never know how she managed to keep herself from doing exactly that.

She wanted it as much as she feared it. The push and pull of that made her feel something like seasick, though that certainly wasn't *nausea* that pooled in her. Not even close.

"I'm not very good at following orders," she managed to say.

There was the faintest suggestion of a curve to that grimly sensual mouth entirely too near her own.

"Not yet, perhaps," he said. "But you will become adept and obedient. I will insist."

Scandalous Sheikh Brides

And the powerful men who claim them!

In their rival desert kingdoms the word of Sheikhs
Rihad and Kavian is law.
Nothing and no one stands in the way of
these formidable and passionate rulers.

Until two exceptional women dare to defy them
and turn their carefully controlled worlds
upside down.

These men will do whatever it takes to protect
their legacies, including claiming these women
as their brides before scandals ensue!

Read Rihad's story in

Protecting the Desert Heir

June 2015

And Kavian and Princess Amaya's story in

Traded to the Desert Sheikh

September 2015

Caitlin Crews

———

Traded to the Desert Sheikh

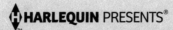
HARLEQUIN PRESENTS®

Recycling programs
for this product may
not exist in your area.

ISBN-13: 978-0-373-13369-7

Traded to the Desert Sheikh

First North American Publication 2015

Copyright © 2015 by Caitlin Crews

Printed in U.S.A.

USA TODAY bestselling and RITA® Award–nominated author **Caitlin Crews** loves writing romance. She teaches her favorite romance novels in creative writing classes at places like UCLA Extension's prestigious Writers' Program, where she finally gets to utilize the MA and PhD in English literature she received from the University of York in England. She currently lives in California with her very own hero and too many pets. Visit her at caitlincrews.com.

Books by Caitlin Crews

Harlequin Presents

At the Count's Bidding
Undone by the Sultan's Touch
Not Just the Boss's Plaything
A Devil in Disguise
In Defiance of Duty
The Replacement Wife
Princess from the Past

The Chatsfield

Greek's Last Redemption

Scandalous Sheikh Brides

Protecting the Desert Heir

Vows of Convenience

His for Revenge
His for a Price

Royal & Ruthless

A Royal Without Rules

Scandal in the Spotlight

No More Sweet Surrender
Heiress Behind the Headlines

Self-Made Millionaires

Katrakis's Last Mistress

Bride on Approval

Pure Princess, Bartered Bride

Visit the Author Profile page
at Harlequin.com for more titles.

CHAPTER ONE

SHE HAD NO WARNING.

There had been no telltale men with grim, assessing eyes watching her from the shadows. No strange gaps in conversation when she walked into the small coffee shop in a tiny lakeside village in British Columbia. There hadn't been any of the usual hang-ups or missed calls on her latest disposable mobile phone that signaled her little noose was drawing tight.

She had a large mug of strong, hot coffee to ward off the late-autumn chill this far north, where snow was plastered across the Canadian Rocky Mountains and the thick clouds hung low. The pastry she chose was cloyingly sweet, but she ate all of it anyway. She checked her email, her messages. There was a new voice mail from her older brother, Rihad, which she ignored. She would call him later, when she was less exposed. When she could be certain Rihad's men couldn't track her.

And then she glanced up, some disturbance in the air around her making her skin draw tight in the second before *he* took the seat across from her at the tiny little café table.

"Hello, Amaya," he said, with a kind of calm, resolute satisfaction—while everything inside her shifted into one great big scream. "You've been more difficult to find than anticipated."

As if this were a perfectly casual meeting, here in this quiet café in an off-season lakeside village in a remote part of Canada she'd been certain he couldn't find. As if he weren't the most dangerous man in the world to her—this man who held her life in those hands of his that looked so easy and idle on the table between them despite their scars and marks of hard use, in notable contrast to that dark slate fury in his too-gray eyes.

As if she hadn't left him—His Royal Highness, Kavian ibn Zayed al Talaas, ruling sheikh of the desert stronghold Daar Talaas—if not precisely at the altar, then pretty damn close six months ago.

Amaya had been running ever since. She'd survived on the money in her wallet and her ability to leave no trail, thanks to a global network of friends and acquaintances she'd met throughout her vagabond youth at her heart-broken mother's side. She'd crashed on the floors of perfect strangers, stayed in the forgotten rooms of friends of friends and walked miles upon miles in the pitch dark to get out of cities and even countries where she'd thought he might have tracked her. She wanted nothing more than to leap up and run now, down the streets of the near-deserted village of Kaslo and straight into the frigid waters of Lake Kootenay if necessary—but she had absolutely no doubt that if she tried that again, Kavian would catch her.

With his own bare hands this time.

And she couldn't repress the shiver that swept over her at that thought.

Much less the one that chased it, when Kavian's sensually grim mouth curved slightly at the sight of her reaction.

Control yourself, she snapped. Inside her own head.

But Kavian looked as if he heard that, too. She hated that some part of her believed that he could.

"You seem surprised to see me," he said. "Surely not."

"Of course I'm surprised." Amaya didn't know how she managed to push the words out of her mouth. A list of things she needed to do—right that second, if there was any hope for her to escape him again now that he'd be fully expecting her to try—raced through her head. But she couldn't seem to look away from him. Just like the last time she'd met him, at her brother's palace to the south of Kavian's desert kingdom, for the occasion of her arranged engagement to this man, Kavian commanded her full attention. "I thought the last six months made it clear that I didn't want to see you, ever again."

"You belong to me," he said, with that same sheer certainty that had sent ice spearing through her at the celebration of their betrothal in the Bakrian Royal Palace half a year ago. That same spear felt even colder now. "Was this moment truly in doubt? I was always going to find you, Amaya. The only question was when."

His voice was deceptively calm, something like silken in the quiet of the small café. It did nothing to lessen the humming sort of threat that emanated from that lethal body of his, all harsh muscle and a kind of lean, austere maleness that was as foreign to her as it was oddly, disruptively fascinating. He looked nothing like the local men who had been in and out of this very café all morning, wreathed in hearty beards and thick plaid jackets to fend off the northern cold.

Kavian wore unrelenting black, relieved only by those furious slate-gray eyes he didn't shift from her for a single moment. Black trousers on his tough, strong legs, utilitarian black boots on his feet. What looked like a fine black T-shirt beneath the black bomber jacket he wore half-zipped that managed to show off his granite-hard chest rather than conceal it in any way. His thick dark hair was shorter than she remembered it, and the closer-cut style accentuated the deadly lines of his brutally captivating face, from that warrior's jaw with the faintest hint of his dark beard as if he hadn't bothered to shave in days, his blade of a nose and cheekbones male models would have died for that nonetheless looked like weapons on such a hard-hewn face.

He looked like an assassin, not a king. Or perhaps a king in hiding as some kind of nightmare. *Her* nightmare. Either way, he looked catastrophically out of place here, so far across the planet from Daar Talaas, where his rule seemed as natural as the desolate desert and the stark, forbidding mountains that dominated his remote country.

Or perhaps the only catastrophe was the way her heart thundered inside her chest, louder by the second. He was like a shot of unwanted, far-too-tactile memory and adrenaline mixed into one, reminding her of the treacherous, unwelcoming desert where she'd been born and where she'd spent the first few years of her life, wrapped up tight in all that sweltering heat, storming sand and blinding, terrible light.

Amaya hated the desert.

She told herself she wasn't any fonder of Kavian.

"You are quite enterprising."

She didn't think that was a compliment. Not exactly. Not from this man, with his harsh gaze and that assessing way he looked at her, as if he was sizing her up for structural weaknesses he could then set about exploiting for his own ends. *That's exactly what he's doing*, she told herself.

"We almost had you in Prague two months ago."

"Unlikely, as I was never in Prague."

That crook of his mouth again, that made her breath feel choppy and her lips sting, and Amaya was certain he knew full well that she was lying.

"Are you proud of yourself?" he asked. She noticed then

that he hadn't moved in all the time he'd sat there. That he remained too still, too watchful. Like a sentry. Or a sniper. "You have caused untold damage with this pointless escapade of yours. The scandal alone could topple two kingdoms and yet here you sit, happy to lie to my face and sip at a latte in the wilds of Canada as if you are a stranger to your own responsibilities."

There was no reason that should hit Amaya like a blow.

She was the half sister of the current king of Bakri, it was true. But she hadn't been raised in the palace or even in the country, as some kind of royal princess draped in tiaras and expectations. Her mother had taken Amaya with her when she left and then divorced the former king— Amaya's father—and Amaya had been raised in her mother's painful whirlwind of a wake. A season here, a season there. Yachts in the south of France or Miami, artistic communes in places like Taos, New Mexico, or the beach resorts of Bali. Glitzy cities bristling with the rich and famous in their high-class penthouses and hotel suites, distant ranches ringed with fat, sleek cattle and more rustic interpretations of excessive wealth. Wherever the wind had blown Elizaveta al Bakri, wherever there were people to adore her appropriately and pay for the privilege, which Amaya had come to understand was her mother's substitute for the love her father hadn't given her, that was where they'd gone—as long as it was never, ever back to Bakri, the scene of the crime as far as Elizaveta was concerned.

That Amaya had returned to the country of her birth at all, much less because Rihad had prevailed upon her after their father had died and somehow gotten into her head with his talk of *her birthright*, had caused a distinct rift between Amaya and her mother. Elizaveta had been noticeably frosty to her only child since the old king's funeral, which Amaya had attended and which had been, in Elizaveta's view, a deep betrayal.

Amaya understood. Elizaveta still loved her lost king, Amaya was sure of it. It was just that Elizaveta's thwarted love had grown more than a little gnarled and knotted over all these years, becoming indistinguishable from hate.

But there was no point thinking about her complicated relationship with her mother, much less her mother's even more complicated relationship with emotions. It solved nothing—especially not Amaya's current predicament. Or what Kavian viewed as her *responsibilities*.

"You're talking about my brother's responsibilities," Amaya said now, somehow holding Kavian's hard warrior gaze steadily as if she weren't in the least moved by his appearance before her. It she did it long enough, maybe she'd believe it herself. "Not mine."

"Six months ago, I was prepared to be patient with you." His voice was soft. It was the only thing about him that was. "I was not unaware of the way you were raised, so ignorant of your own history and the ancient ways, forever on the run. I knew this union would present challenges for you. Six months ago, I intended to meet those challenges as civilly and carefully as possible."

The world, so still already since he'd sat across from her, shrank down until it was nothing but that flame of sheer, crackling temper in his dangerous gaze. Gray and fierce. Piercing into her, beneath her skin, like a terrible burning she could neither control nor extinguish. It seared through her, rolling too fast, too unchecked, too massive to bear.

"How thoughtful you were six months ago," she said faintly. "It's funny how you didn't mention any of that at the time. You were too busy posturing and grandstanding with my brother. Playing to the press. I was nothing more than a little bit of set dressing at my own engagement party."

"Are you as vain as your mother before you, then?" His voice turned so hard it left her feeling hollow, as if it had punched straight through her, though he still didn't move at all. "That is a great pity. The desert is not kind to vanity, you will find. It will strip you down to the bone and leave only who you really are behind, whether you are ready to face that harsh truth or not."

Something flickered behind that fierce gaze of his, she thought—though she didn't want to know what it was, what it meant. She didn't want to imagine who he *really* was. Not when he was so overwhelming already.

"You paint such a lovely picture," she threw back at him. She didn't understand why she was still sitting there, doing nothing but chatting with him. *Chatting.* Why did she feel paralyzed when he was near? The same thing had happened the last time, at their celebration six months ago. And then far worse—but she refused to think about that. Not here. Not now, with him watching her. "Who wouldn't want to race off to the desert right now on such a delightful voyage of self-discovery?"

Kavian moved then, and that was worse than his alarming stillness. Far worse. He rose to his feet with a lethal show of grace that made Amaya's temples pound, her throat go dry. Then he reached down, took her hand without asking or even hesitating and pulled her to her feet.

And the insane part was that she went.

She didn't fight. She didn't recoil. She didn't even *try.* His hand was calloused and rough against hers, hot and strong, and her stomach flipped, then dropped. Her toes arched in the boots she wore. She came up too fast and once again, found herself teetering too close to this man. This stranger she could not, would not marry.

This man she could not think about without that answering fire so deep within.

"Let go of me," she whispered.

"What will you do if I do not?"

His voice was still calm, but she was closer to him now, and she felt the rumble of it like a deep bass line inside her. His skin was the color of cinnamon, and heat seemed to blast from him, from his hand around hers and his face bent toward her. He was bigger than she was, tall enough that her head reached only his shoulder, and the fact that he'd spent his whole life training in the art of war was like a living flame between them. It was written deep into every proud inch of him. She could see the white line of an old scar etched across the proud column of his throat, and refused to let herself think about how he might have come by it.

He was a war machine, this man. *Kavian is of the old school, in every meaning of the term*, her brother had told her. She'd known that going in. She couldn't pretend otherwise.

What she hadn't realized was how it would affect her. It felt as if she were standing too close to a wicked bonfire, her face on the verge of blistering from the intense heat, with no way to tell when the wind might change.

Kavian tugged on her hand, bringing her closer against his chest, then bending his head to speak directly into her ear.

"Will you scream?" he asked softly. Or perhaps it was a taunt. "Cry out for help from all these soft strangers? What do you think will happen if you do? I am not a civilized man, Amaya. I do not live by your rules. I do not care who gets in my way."

And she shook, as much from the sensation of his breath against her ear as the words he used. Or maybe it wasn't either of those—maybe it was that he was holding her against that body of his again, and she was still haunted by what had happened the last time. What she hadn't done a single thing to stop—but that was desert madness, nothing more, she told herself harshly.

She had no choice but to believe that. It was the only thing that made any sense.

"I believe you," she hissed at him. "But I doubt that you want to end up on the evening news, uncivilized or not. That would be a bit too much scandal, I think we can agree."

"Is this a theory you truly wish to test?"

She yanked herself back from him, out of his grip, and it wasn't lost on her that he let her go. That he had been in control of her since the moment he walked into this café—or before, she realized as her stomach flipped over inside her again and then slammed down at her feet. It must have been before.

Amaya looked around a little bit wildly and realized—belatedly—that the café was unusually empty for the early afternoon. The handful of locals who remained seemed to have studiously averted their gazes in a way that suggested someone had either told them to do so or compensated them for it. And she could see the two brawny men, also in head-to-toe, relentless black, standing at the front door like sentries and worse, the sleek black SUV idling at the curb outside. Waiting.

For her.

She jerked her gaze back to Kavian. "How long have you been following me?"

His dark eyes gleamed.

"Since we located you in Mont-Tremblant, all the way across this great, wide country in Quebec ten days ago." Kavian was calm, of course. But then, he'd already won.

Why wouldn't he be calm? "You should not have returned there if you truly wished to remain at large."

"I was only there for three days." She frowned at him. "Three days in six months."

He only gazed back at her as if he were made entirely of stone and could do so forever—and would, if it was required. As if he were a monolith and as movable.

"Mont-Tremblant was your favorite of the upscale ski resorts your mother preferred whenever her winter tastes ran to cold weather and ski chalets. I assume that played a part in why you opted to go to university in Montreal, so you could better access it in your free time. I've long suspected that if you were likely to return to any of the places your mother dragged you over the years, it would be there."

"How long have you been *studying* me?" Amaya managed to scrape out, her heart right there in her throat. She was surprised he couldn't see it.

And Kavian smiled then, a quirk of his absurdly compelling mouth that made her doubt her own sanity. But there was no doubting the way it wound in her, tightening the knot in her belly, making her feel unsteady on her feet.

She had the strangest notion that he knew it.

"I don't think you're ready to hear that," he told her, and there was something else, then, in those slate-gray eyes. Inhabiting that warrior's face of his, stone and steel. And he was right, she thought. She didn't want to hear it. "Not here. Not now."

"I think I deserve to know exactly how much of an obsessed stalker you are, in fact. So I can prepare myself accordingly."

He almost laughed. She saw the silver of it in his gaze, in the movement of that mouth of his, though he made no sound.

"What you deserve is to be thrown over my shoulder

and bodily removed from this establishment." She'd never heard him sound anything but supernaturally calm and almost hypnotic in his intensity, and so that rough edge to his voice then shocked her. It made her jolt to attention, her eyes flying wide on his. "Make no mistake. If I'd caught up to you in a less stuffy place than Canada, we wouldn't be bothering with polite conversation at all. My patience ran out six months ago, Amaya."

"You threaten me, and then you wonder why I ran?"

"I don't care why you ran," he replied, ruthless and swift, and she'd never heard him sound quite like that, either. "You can walk outside and get in that car, or I can put you there. Your choice."

"I don't understand this." She did nothing to hide the bitterness in her voice, the anguish that she'd walked into this trap six months ago thinking her eyes were open, or the fear that she'd never get out of it again. "You could have any other woman in the world as your queen. I'm sure there are millions who lie awake at night dreaming of coronations and crowns. And you could certainly ally your country to my brother's if that was what you wanted, whether or not your queen was related to him. You don't need me."

Again, that smile, dangerous and compelling and world-altering at once. The essence of Kavian, boiled down to that small quirk of his too-hard mouth.

"But I want you," he said, deep and certain. So very certain, like stone. "So it amounts to the same thing."

Kavian thought for a moment she would bolt, despite the obvious futility of another such attempt.

And that wildness that was always a part of him, the desert that lived inside him, untamed and unconquerable and darker than the night, wished that she'd try. Because he was not the kind of man she'd known all her life. He was not pallid and weak, Western and accommodating. He had been forged in steel and loss, had struck down treachery and rebellion alike with his own two bloodstained hands. He had made himself what he most hated because it had been a necessary evil, a burden he'd been prepared to shoulder for the good of his people. Perhaps it had been too easy a transition; perhaps he *was* the darkness itself—but those were questions for a restless soul, a long, dark night. Kavian had never been a good man, only a determined one.

He would not only chase her to ground; he would enjoy it.

Something of that must have showed on his face because she paled, his runaway princess who had evaded him all this time and in so doing, proved herself the very queen she claimed she didn't want to become. The very queen he needed.

And then she swallowed so hard he could hear it and, beast that he was, he liked that, too.

"Run," he invited her, the way he'd once invited a challenger to attempt to take his throne. With untrained hands and an unwieldy ego. It had not ended well for that foolish upstart. To say nothing of the traitorous creature who had struck down Kavian's father before him. Kavian was not a good man. The woman who would become his queen should have no doubts on that score. "See what happens."

He didn't know what he expected her to do, but it wasn't that defiant glare she aimed at him, her hands fisted on her hips, as if she was considering taking a swing at him right there in public. He wished she'd do that, too. Any touch at all, he'd take.

She was so pretty that she should have been spoiled and delicate, a fragile glass thing better kept high on a soft, safe shelf—and he'd thought she was. He would have worshipped her as such. That she was *this*, as well—with the ingenuity to hide from him for this long and the sheer strength to stand before him without shrinking or collapsing when many grown men did not dare do the same—came far too close to making him…furious.

Well. Perhaps *furious* was not quite the correct term. But it was dark, that ribbon of reaction in him. Supple and lush. And it gripped him like a slick vise all the same. He imagined it was a kind of admiration. For the fierce and worthy queen she would become, if he could but tame her to the role. Kavian had no doubt that he could do it, in time. That he would.

Had he not done everything he'd ever set out to do, no matter how treacherous the path? What was one woman next to a throne reclaimed, a family avenged, the stain on his soul? Even if it was this one. This woman, who fought him where others only cowered.

God help him but he liked it. The angrier she made him with her defiance, the more he liked her.

Her beauty had been a hammer to the side of his head from the start, taking him by surprise. His first inkling that he, too, was a mortal man who could be toppled by the same sins as any other. It had not been a revelation he had particularly enjoyed. He could remember all too well that meeting with Rihad al Bakri, the other man at that time merely the heir apparent to the Bakrian throne.

"You want an alliance," he'd said when Rihad was brought before him in the grand, bejeweled throne room in the old city of Daar Talaas that had been hewn into the rocks themselves and for centuries had stood as a great stronghold. Kavian wanted to make certain it would stand for centuries more.

"I do."

"What benefit is there in such an alliance for me?"

Rihad had talked at length about politics and the drums of war that beat so long and so hard in their part of the world that Kavian had started to consider it their own form of regional music. And it was far better to dance than to die. Moreover, he'd known Rihad was correct—the mighty powers around them imposed their rule by greed and cunning and, when that did not work, the long-range missiles of their foreign-funded militaries. In this way, the world was still won, day after bloody day.

"And I have a sister," Rihad had said, at the end of this trip through unsavory political realities.

"Many men have sisters. Not all of those men also have kingdoms in peril that could use the support of my army."

Because Daar Talaas might not have been as well funded as some of their neighbors, nor was its military as vast, but they had not been beaten by a single foreign force since they had ousted the last Ottoman sultanate in the fifteenth century.

"You strike me as a man who prefers the old ways." Rihad had shrugged, though his gaze had been shrewd. "Surely there remains no better way to unite two families, or two countries, than to become one in fact."

"Says the man who has not offered to marry my sister," Kavian had murmured, lounging there on his throne as if he hadn't cared one way or the other. "Though it is his kingdom that hangs in the balance."

Rihad had not replied with the obvious retort, that Kavian had no sisters and that his brothers had been taken out much too young in the bloody coup Kavian's predecessor had led. Instead, he'd handed over a tablet computer and had pressed Play on the cued-up video.

"My sister," he'd said. Simply enough.

She'd been pretty, of course. But Kavian had been surrounded by pretty women his whole life. Supplicants presented them to him like desserts for him to choose between, or simply collect. His harem had been stocked with the finest selection of feminine beauty from all over his lands, and even beyond.

But this one was something else.

It was the perfect oval of her face and that lush, carnal mouth of hers as she'd talked back to Rihad in a manner that could only have been described as challenging. Defiant. Not in the least bit docile, and Kavian found he liked it far too much.

It was the thick, lustrously dark hair she'd plaited to one side and thrown over one of her smooth shoulders, covered only by the faintest thin straps of the pale white tank top she wore that drew attention to her olive skin even as it was perfectly clear that she'd given her appearance little to no thought. It was the crackling energy and bright, gleaming light in her faintly Eurasian eyes, the color of bittersweet chocolates ringed in fancifully dark lashes, that inspired a man to look again, to look closer, to do what he could to never look away.

And it was what she was saying, in that slightly husky voice with an unplaceable accent, neither North American nor European, not quite. She'd used her hands for emphasis, and animated facial expressions besides, instead of the studied, elegant placidity of the women he knew. She'd talked so quickly, so passionately, that he'd been interested despite himself. And when she finished, she'd laughed, and it had been like clear, cool water. Sparkling and bright, washing him clean, and making him thirsty— so very, very thirsty—for more.

"Let me guess," she'd said, her voice dry and faintly teasing in a way that had shot straight to the hardest part of him—forcing Kavian to remind himself that she hadn't been speaking to *him*. That what he'd been watching was a taped video call between this woman and her brother. "The mighty King of Bakri is not a Harry Potter fan."

She had been a hard blow to his temple, making his head spin. The effect of such an unexpected hit had coursed through his body like some kind of ferocious virus, burning away everything in its path and leaving only one word behind:

Mine.

But he'd only smiled blandly at Rihad when the video finished.

"I am not at all certain I require a wife at present," he'd said languidly, and the negotiation had begun.

He'd never imagined it would lead him here, to this inhospitable land of snow and ice, pine trees and heavy fog, so far north he could feel the chill of winter like a dull metal deep in his bones. He admired her defiance. He craved it. It would make her the perfect queen to reign at his side. But he also needed a wife who would obey him.

Men like his own father had handled these competing needs by taking more than one wife—one for each required role. But Kavian would not make his father's mistakes. He was certain he could find everything he needed in one woman. In this woman.

"Listen to me," Amaya was saying, her hands still on her hips, her defiant chin high, as if this were another negotiation instead of a foregone conclusion. "If you'd listened to me in the first place, none of this would have happened."

"I have listened to you." He had listened to her back in Bakri, or he'd intended to listen to her anyway, and then she'd run. What benefit was there in listening any further? Her actions had spoken for her, clear and unmistakable.

"The next time I listen to you, it will be in the old city, where you can run your heart out for miles in all directions and find nothing but the desert and my men. I will listen and listen, if I must. And it will all end the same way. You will be beneath me and all of this will have been a pointless exercise in the inevitable."

CHAPTER TWO

KAVIAN TURNED THEN and started for the door, aware that all the exits were blocked by his men on the off chance she was foolish enough to try to escape him one last time.

He still hoped she would. He truly did. The beast in him yearned for that chase.

"We are leaving, Amaya. One way or the other. If you wish me to force you, I am happy to oblige. I am not from your world. The only rules I follow are the ones I make."

He yanked open the door and let the sharp weather in, nodding to the guards who waited for him on the other side. Then he looked back at this woman who did not seem to realize that she'd been his all along.

That all she was doing was delaying what had always been coming, as surely as the stars followed the setting sun. As surely as he had assumed the mantle of his enemy to defeat the murderous interloper and reclaim his throne, no matter the personal cost or the dark stain it left behind.

Her hands had dropped from her hips and were balled into fists at her sides, and even in the face of her pointless stubbornness he found her beautiful. Shockingly so. He could still feel that resounding blow to the side of his skull, making the world ring and whirl all around him.

And this despite the fact that she still wore her hair in that same impatient braid, a long, messy tail pulled forward over one shoulder as if she hadn't wanted to bother with it any further. At their engagement party, she'd worn it up high in too many braids to count, woven together into some kind of elegant crown. And here he stood on the other side of the world, still itching to undo it all himself and let the heavy, dark length of it fall free.

He wanted to bury himself in the slippery silk of it, the fragrant warmth. In her, any way he could have her. *Every* way.

It didn't even matter that she was dressed in a manner that did not suit her fine, delicately otherworldly allure— and was certainly not appropriate for a woman who would be his queen. Jeans that were entirely too formfitting for eyes that were not his. Markedly unfeminine boots. Both equally scuffed and lived in, as if she were still the university student she'd been not too long ago. A bulky sweatshirt that hid her figure, save those long and slender legs of hers that nothing could conceal and that he wanted wrapped around him. And the puffy jacket she'd thrown over the nearest chair when she sat down that, when she wore it zipped up to her chin, made her look almost like a perfect circle above the waist.

Kavian wanted to wrap her in silks and drape her in jewels. He wanted her to stand tall beside him. He wanted to decorate her in nothing but delicate gold chains and build whole palaces in her name, as the ancient sultans had done for the women who'd captivated them. He wanted her strength as much as her beauty.

He wanted to explore every inch of her sweet body with his battered hands, his warrior's body, his mouth, his tongue.

But first, and foremost, he wanted to take her home.

"Is it force, then?" he asked her, standing in the open doorway, not in the least bit concerned about being overheard by the townspeople. "Will I throw you over my shoulder like the barbarians of old? I think you know I will not hesitate to do exactly that. And enjoy it."

She shuddered then and he would have given his kingdom, in that moment, to know whether it was desire or revulsion that swept through her at that thought. He hated that he didn't know her well enough, yet, to tell the difference.

That, too, would change. And far quicker than it might have had she come with him as she'd been meant to do the night of their engagement party, when he'd been predisposed toward a gentler understanding of her predicament. But there was nothing gentle left in him. He had become stone.

Amaya swept her big coat up in one hand and hung the ratty bag she carried over one shoulder. But she still didn't move toward him.

"If I come with you now," she said, that husky voice of hers very even, very low, "you have to promise that you won't—"

"No."

She blinked. "You don't know what I was going to say."

"What can it matter? I made you a set of promises upon our betrothal. You should not require anything further. You made me promises, too, Amaya, which you broke that very same night. It is better, I think, that you and I do not dwell on promises."

"But—"

"This is not a debate," he said gently, but he could see the way the edge beneath it slapped at her.

Her lips fell open, as if she had to breathe hard to get through that slap, and he couldn't pretend he didn't approve of the way she did it. She even stood taller. He liked that she was beautiful, of course he did. Kavian was a man, after all. A flesh-and-blood king who knew full well the benefits of such beauty when he could display it on his arm. But his queen had to be strong or, like his own fragile and ultimately treacherous mother, she would never survive the rigors of their life together. She would dissolve at the first hint of a storm, and he couldn't have that.

Life was storms, not sunshine. The latter was a gift. It was not reality.

Kavian was a warrior king. Amaya had to be a warrior queen, in her own way. No matter how little she liked the lessons that would make her into what he needed.

He was certain he, at least, would enjoy them.

"There are no caveats, no negotiations," he told her. Perhaps too firmly. "You have no choices here. Only an option regarding the delivery method toward the same end."

He thought she would argue, because it seemed she always argued—and, of course, when he'd elected to quiet her in the only other way he knew, she'd bolted for six months. He could admire it now that it was over. Now that she was in his possession, where she belonged.

But today, his warrior queen lifted her head high and walked toward him instead, her dark chocolate gaze cool on his.

"That sounds ominous," she said. Still, she walked through the door of her own volition, out into the moody light of this cold northern morning. "Will you throw a potato sack over my head? Keep my mouth shut with duct tape? Make this a good old-fashioned sort of kidnapping?"

Kavian probably shouldn't have found that amusing. He was aware that was begging for trouble, but he couldn't help it, especially not when she walked out in front of him and he understood, at last, the true benefit of a tight pair of jeans on a fine-figured woman.

His palms ached with the urge to test the shape of

that bottom of hers, to haul her against him the way he had done but once, six months ago. It hadn't been nearly enough, no matter how many times he'd replayed it while scouring the earth for her trail.

"It is a relatively short helicopter flight to Calgary," he said. "Then a mere fifteen hours or so to Daar Talaas. It is entirely up to you if you wish to dress in sacks and tape. I can drug you, if that will appeal to your sense of victimization. Whatever you wish, my queen, it shall be yours."

She stopped then, on the street in this small little Western town in the middle of so much towering wilderness. She turned slowly, as if she was still processing that dry tone of his, and when she met his gaze her own was solemn.

"I can't be your queen," she said quietly. "You must know that. Surely that, if nothing else, became clear to you over all these months."

He didn't try to keep his hands off her, then. He pulled that thick plait into his palm and let the warm silk gently abrade his skin. It wasn't lost on him that if he wished it, he could tug her closer to him, hold her fast, use that braid to help him plunder that plump mouth of hers. The specter of that possibility danced between them and he knew, somehow, that those dark, greedy moments in her brother's palace hung there, too. Steaming up the cold air. Making her cheeks bloom red and his blood heat.

"You promised yourself to me," he reminded her. "You made oaths and I accepted them. You gave yourself into my hands, Amaya. You can confuse this issue with as many words as you like—forced betrothal, political engagement, arranged marriage. Whatever way you hedge a bet in this strange place and pretend a promise need not be kept. In my world, you belong to me already. You have been mine for months."

"I don't accept that," Amaya whispered, but he was attuned to what she didn't do. She didn't weep. She didn't pull away. She didn't so much as avert her gaze. He felt all of those things like caresses.

"I don't require your acceptance," he said softly. "I only require you."

There were no direct routes into the ancient desert city that comprised the central stronghold—and royal palace—of Daar Talaas. It had been a myth, a legend, for many centuries, whispered about by traders and defeated challengers to its throne, incorporated into battle songs and epic poems. In these modern times, satellites and spy drones and online travelogues made certain there was no possibility of truly hiding a whole city away from the rest of the world, but that didn't mean the old royal seat of the warrior kings of Daar Talaas was any more accessible for being known.

The roads only led an hour or so into the desert from any given border, then ended abruptly, unmarked and nowhere near the city itself. There was nothing but the shifting desert sands in the interior of the country, with secret and hard-to-find tunnels beneath the formidable mountains that the natives had used to evade potential invaders for centuries. There were other, somewhat more modern places in the country that appeared on all the maps and were easily approached by anyone insane enough to consider the wide, empty desert a reasonable destination— but the ancient seat of Daar Talaas's power remained half mystery, half mirage.

Almost impossible to attack by land.

Much less escape.

She might not ever have wanted to end up in this place, Amaya reflected as she stepped out of the small, sleek jet into the bright, hot desert heat and the instantly parching slap of the wind that went with it, but that didn't mean she hadn't studied up on it. Just in case.

Kavian moved behind, shepherding her down the stairs toward the dusty tarmac as if he imagined she really might fling aside her jet lag and race off into the treacherous embrace of the shifting, beckoning sand. And after fifteen hours in an enclosed space with all that sensual menace that blazed from him like a radiator in the depths of a Canadian winter, Amaya was almost crazed enough to consider it.

"I won't even send my guards after you," he murmured, sounding both much too close and entirely amused, as if reading her mind or the longing in that glance she'd aimed at the horizon was funny. "I'll run you down myself. I'm not afraid to tackle a woman, particularly not when she has proved as slippery as you have. And imagine what might happen then?"

She didn't have to imagine it. She'd spent a large portion of her time and energy these past six months doing her best to cast the memory of that night at her brother's palace out of her head.

"That will never happen again," she assured him.

His hand curled around the nape of her neck as her feet hit the ground. He didn't release her as he stepped into place beside her; if anything, his hand tightened. He leaned in close, letting his lips brush against her cheek, and Amaya was certain he knew exactly what that did to her. How the heat of it rushed over her as if she'd dropped off the side of the parched earth into a boiling sea. How her skin pulled tight and her breasts seemed to swell. How her breath caught and her core melted.

Of course he knew. He remembered, too. She had no doubt.

"It will happen often," he said, warning and promise at once, "and soon."

Amaya shuddered, and she couldn't convince herself it was entirely fear. But he only laughed, low and entirely too lethal. He didn't let go of her until he'd helped her into the waiting helicopter and started to buckle her in himself.

"I'm not going to fling myself out of a moving helicopter," she gritted out at him, only *just* stopping herself from batting at those fascinatingly male hands of his as they moved efficiently over her, tugging here and snapping there, and managing to kick up new brush fires as if he'd used his teeth against the line of her neck.

He eyed her in that disconcertingly frank way of his that made something low and hot inside her constrict, then flip.

"Not now, no," he agreed.

It was a quick, dizzying ride. They shot up high into the air in a near-vertical lift, and then flew over the nearest steep and forbidding mountain range to drop down in a tumultuous rush on the other side.

Amaya had a disjointed, roller-coaster sense of a city piled high along the walls of a deep, jagged valley, the stacked buildings made of smooth, ancient stone that seemed almost a part of the mountains themselves. There were spires and minarets, flags snapping briskly against the wind, smooth domes and thick, sturdy walls that reminded her of nothing so much as a fort. She had the impression of leafy green squares tucked away from the sprawl of the desert, of courtyards bursting with bright and fanciful flowers, and then they touched down and Kavian's hands were on her again.

She started to protest but bit it off when she looked at the expression on his hard face. It was too triumphant. Too darkly intent.

He'd promised her months ago that he would bring her

home to his palace, and now he had done so. Her throat went dry as he herded her off the helicopter with him—she told herself it was the desert air, though she knew better—as she wondered exactly how many of his promises she could expect him to keep.

All of them, a small voice deep inside her intoned, like a death knell. *You know he will keep every single promise he ever made to you.*

She had to repress an involuntary shiver at that, but they'd stepped out onto a breezy rooftop and there was no time and certainly no space to indulge her apprehension. Kavian wrapped his hard fingers around her wrist and pulled her along with him as he moved, not adjusting his stride in the least to accommodate hers.

And she would die before she'd ask him to do so.

They'd landed on the very top of a grand structure cut into the highest part of this side of the valley, Amaya comprehended in the few moments before they moved inside. And then they were walking down a complicated series of sweeping, marbled stairs and through royal halls inlaid with jaw-droppingly beautiful mosaics, lovingly crafted into high arches and soaring ceilings. Though they'd gone inside, there was no sense of closeness; the palace was bright and open, with light pouring in from all directions, making Amaya feel dizzy all over again as she tried to work out the systems of skylights and arched windows that made a palace of rock feel this airy.

People she was dimly aware were various members of his staff moved toward him and around him, taking instruction and carrying on rapid-fire conversations with him as he strode deeper and deeper into the palace complex without so much as a hitch in that stride of his. They all spoke in the Arabic she'd learned as a child, that she still knew enough of to work out the basic meaning of what was said around her, if not every word or nuance. Something about the northern border. Something about a ceremony. An aside about what sounded like housekeeping, a subject she was surprised a king—especially a king as inaccessibly mighty as Kavian—spent any time thinking about in the first place. Each aide would approach him, walk with him briefly and deferentially, then fall back again as if each were a part of the royal wake he left behind him as he charged through his ornate and bejeweled world, never so much as pausing as he went.

That was Kavian. She'd understood it six months ago, on a deep and visceral level. She understood it even more clearly now. He was a brutal force, focused and unstoppable. He took what he wanted. He did not hesitate.

It took her a shuddering sort of moment to recognize it when he finally did stop walking, and even then, it was only because he finally let go of her arm. She couldn't help putting her hands to her stomach as if she could stop the way it flipped and rolled, or make her lungs take in a little more air.

First she realized they were all alone. Then she glanced around.

It seemed as if they stood in an enormous cavern, lit by lanterns in the scattered seating areas and sconces in the stone walls, though she could see, far on the other side of the great space, what looked like another open courtyard bathed in the bright desert light. It took Amaya another moment or two to notice the pools of water laid out in a kind of circle around the central seating and lounging area where they stood. Some steaming, some not. And all the fountains that poured into them from a dragon's mouth here, a lion's mouth there, carved directly into the stone walls.

"Where are we?" she asked.

Her voice resounded in the space, coming back a damp echo, and smaller, somehow, than she'd meant it to sound.

And Kavian stood there before her, his arms crossed over his magnificent black-covered chest with the gleaming pools all around him, and smiled.

"These are the harem baths."

There was something sour in her mouth then. "The harem."

"The baths, yes. The harem itself comprises many more rooms, suites, courtyards. A whole wing of the palace, as you will discover."

"It's empty." Amaya forced herself to look around to confirm that, and hated that she was afraid she was wrong. She didn't particularly want his attention anyway, did she? What did it matter if it was shared with the other women who must surely be around here somewhere? Her father had been the same kind of man. She'd lived the first eight years of her life in his palace, with his other women in addition to her mother, each one of them one more lash of pain Elizaveta still carried with her today. *Loving a man like your father is losing yourself,* her mother had taught her, *and then watching him lavish his attentions on others instead, while what remains of you shrivels up and dies.* Amaya shouldn't have been surprised, surely, that Kavian was cut from similar cloth. "Surely it can't be a harem without…a harem."

Again, that dark, assessing look of his that she worried could separate her flesh from her bones as easily as it bored inside her head.

"Do you not recall the conversation we had in your brother's palace?"

She wished she didn't. She wished she could block that entire night out of her head, but she'd tried. She'd tried for six months with little success. "No."

"I think you do, Amaya. And I think you have become far too comfortable with the lies you tell. To yourself. To me."

"Or perhaps I simply don't remember, without any grand conspiracy." But her voice was much too hoarse then and she saw that he knew it. Those eyes of his gleamed silver. "Perhaps I didn't find a conversation with you all that interesting. Blasphemous, I know."

"You told me, with all the blustering self-righteousness of your youth and ignorance and many years in North America, that you could not possibly consider marrying a man with a harem, as if such a thing was beneath you when you were born in one yourself. And I told you that for you, I would empty mine." His mouth crooked again, but she felt it like a dark, sensual threat, not a smile. "Does that jog your memory? Or should I remind you what we were doing when I made this promise?"

Amaya looked away, blindly, as if she could make sense of this. What he'd told her then, when she'd been shooting off her mouth to cover the tumult he'd caused inside her. What he appeared to be telling her now.

"I didn't think you really had a harem." She didn't want to look at him again. She didn't want to see the truth on that face of his that had yet to soften a single blow for her, and she really didn't want to question why she should care either way. "My brother doesn't have a harem."

"Neither do I." He waited until, despite herself, she looked at him again as if magnetically drawn to him. As if he controlled her will as easily as he controlled her body. "I haven't had a harem for the past six months. You are welcome."

Amaya blinked, and tried to process that. All its implications.

As if he saw some of that internal struggle on her face,

Kavian laughed, which hardly helped anything. He moved away from her, toward the nearby seating area that dominated the central expanse in the middle of the pools, all stone benches and bright floor pillows around graceful round tables covered in trays of food she didn't want to look at, because she didn't want to eat anything. She didn't want to be here at all.

Amaya had read entirely too many ancient myths in her time. She knew how this went. A few pomegranate seeds and she'd find herself forced to spend half her life trapped in the underworld with the King of Hell. *No, thank you.*

She refused to accept that this was her fate, like her mother's before her. *She refused.*

So she didn't follow him. She didn't dare move a muscle. She was afraid that if she did, the graceful, high ceilings would crash down and pin her here, trapping her forever.

Or maybe she was afraid of something else entirely— and of naming it, too, because she knew exactly where this ended. She'd witnessed it as a child. She'd lived through its aftermath. It didn't matter how hard her heart beat. She knew better.

"How many women did you keep here?" She meant to sound arch and amused, a great sophisticate who could handle what was happening here and the fact of *a harem,* but that wasn't at all how it came out. She felt the searing look he threw her way, though she didn't dare look over at him, felt it sweep over her skin, making her wish she hadn't discarded all her winter outer layers on the plane. Making her wish there was some greater barrier between them than the simple, too-sheer T-shirt she wore.

"Seventeen."

"Seven—you're messing with me, aren't you? Is this your version of teasing?"

"Do I strike you as a man who teases?" he asked, mildly

enough, yet she could hear the heft of his ruthlessness beneath it, the deadly thrust of his intent, like the rock walls all around them.

"You kept seventeen women locked away here." She felt as if she were in the helicopter again, that wild ride like a slingshot across the mountains. "And you—did you—at night, or whenever, did—"

She couldn't finish.

"Did I have sex with them?" he finished for her, his voice smooth and dark, and it moved in her in all the worst possible places. It made her feel greedy and panicked, exactly the way she'd felt in that terrible alcove in her brother's palace when she lost her mind. And everything else. "Is that what you want to know, Amaya?"

"I don't care," she threw at him. "I don't want to know anything. I don't care what you do."

"Do not ask questions if you cannot handle the answers, because I will not sugarcoat them for you." His voice was so dark, so harsh. Inexorable, somehow, as it wrapped around her. "This is no place for petty jealousies and schoolgirl insecurities. You are the queen of Daar Talaas, not a concubine whose name is known to no one."

She jolted at that, as if he'd electrocuted her. "I'm not the queen of anything!"

And it was as if her body only then realized it could move if it liked and that she wasn't trapped here—not yet—and so she whirled around to face him again.

A mistake.

Kavian had stripped down to boxer briefs that molded to his powerful thighs and made Amaya's head go completely, utterly blank. No harems. No concubines. Nothing but him. *Kavian.*

And when she could think again, it wasn't an improvement. There was still nothing but that vast expanse of his steel-honed chest, ridged and muscled in ways that defied reason, that made her mouth water and her knees feel wobbly. He was beautiful. He was something far more intoxicating than merely *beautiful*, more overwhelming than simply *hard*, and yet he was a harsh and powerful male poetry besides.

Her mouth fell open. Without realizing she'd moved at all, Amaya found her hands clamped tight over her heart as if she was afraid it might burst from her chest.

She was, she realized. She was afraid of exactly that.

"I hope you are finished asking these questions I suspect you already know the answers to, Amaya," Kavian said with that dark, quiet triumph in his voice that washed through her like a caress and made her body feel like someone else's. As if it belonged to him, the way it had once before, and she hated that she couldn't get past that. That she felt indelibly marked by him. Branded straight through to her soul. *Owned* whether she wanted to be or not, no matter that she knew better than to let herself feel such things. "Now take off your clothes."

CHAPTER THREE

AMAYA COULDN'T POSSIBLY have heard him correctly.

"I would strip down all the way myself," he was saying, his eyes never leaving her face as he started toward her again. "But I imagine that if I did so, you would faint dead away. And the marble beneath your feet is very hard. You would hurt yourself."

"I would not faint." She cast about for some way to convince him, then settled on the easiest, most provocative lie. The one most likely to repel a man like him. "I've seen battalions of naked men before as they paraded in and out of my bed. What's one more?"

"No," he replied as he closed the distance between them, and there wasn't the faintest hint of uncertainty on his face, in his hard-edged voice. "You have not."

Amaya's shoulders came up against one of the great stone arches, which was how she realized she'd backed away from him. She'd been too lost in his dark gaze to notice anything else. And then he was in front of her and it took every bit of self-preservation she had left not to let out that high-pitched sound that clamored in her throat, especially when he didn't stop stalking toward her until he was *right there*—

If she breathed out, she would touch the golden expanse of his skin. That glorious, warrior's chest with all those fascinating planes and stone-carved shallows that begged for her fingers to explore. That she hungered to *taste* in ways that made her head spin.

But then, she could hardly breathe as it was.

"I told you to remove your clothes, *azizty.*"

His mouth was so close then. She could feel his breath against her lips, particularly when he said the unfamiliar word she was terribly afraid was some kind of endearment. She was more afraid that she *wanted* it to be an endearment, that she was starting down that slippery slope. She could taste him if she only tipped forward—and she would never know how she managed to keep herself from doing exactly that.

She wanted it as much as she feared it. The push and pull of that made her feel something like seasick, though that certainly wasn't *nausea* that pooled in her. Not even close.

"I'm not very good at following orders," she managed to say.

There was the faintest suggestion of a curve to that grimly sensual mouth, entirely too near her own.

"Not yet, perhaps," he said. "But you will become adept and obedient. I will insist."

Time stopped, taut and desperate in that tiny sliver of space between them, and the past tangled all around the present until she hardly knew what was happening now as opposed to what she remembered from the night of their betrothal ceremony.

She could feel his hands in her hair, holding her elegant upswept braids in his palms, holding her head still as he'd taken her mouth like a starving man, again and again and again in that private corner of the Bakrian Royal Palace where they'd gone to "discuss" the very formal, very public promises they'd made to each other. She could feel him again as she had done so then, hard against her as the rest of the world ignited. She could feel that catapulting passion as it had eaten them both alive and made her into someone wholly new and entirely ungovernable, could feel the way he'd hitched her up between his tough, strong body and the alcove's hard wall, and then—

But that had been six months ago. This was here, now, in a great room of bathing pools and echoes, the ghosts of seventeen harem girls and that silvery awareness in his slate-gray eyes.

Amaya thought he would simply bend forward and take her mouth again, the way he had done then, with that low, animal noise that still thrilled her in the recesses of her own mind, still made her nipples draw tight and her toes curl even in memory—

He didn't.

Instead, he shifted and knelt down before her, making what ought to have been an act of some kind of submission feel instead like its opposite.

She should have felt powerful with him at her feet. Bigger than him at last. Instead, she had never felt more delicate or more precarious, and had never felt he was larger or more intimidating. It didn't make sense.

And her heart stopped pretending that what it was doing was *beating*. It wasn't anything so tame, so controlled. It tried to rocket straight out of her chest.

It took her a confused, breathless moment to realize that he was removing her boots, one at a time, and then peeling off her socks, as well. The cool stone beneath her bare feet was a shock to her system, making her remember herself in a sudden rush, as if Kavian had thrown open a window in all this stone and let a crisp wind in.

She reached over to shove him away from her, or that was what she told herself she meant to do, but it was a mistake. Or maybe she hadn't meant to do anything but touch him, because her hands came up hard against those powerful shoulders, and she couldn't describe what she did then as a *shove*. She couldn't seem to *think*. She couldn't seem to do anything but hold on to all that heat, all that fiercely corded strength, and when he tipped his head back to fix her with one of those unsmiling looks of his that wound deep inside her like some kind of spiked thing, laying her bare, she didn't say a word.

She didn't tell him to stop.

His hands moved to the waistband of her jeans, and the denim was shoved down around her thighs before she took another breath, then around her ankles. And she still didn't tell him to stop.

"Please," she said as his big hands wrapped around her ankles, when it was much too late. "I can't."

But she didn't know what she meant. And he wasn't caressing her; he was undressing her with a ruthless efficiency that stunned her into incoherence. He surged to his feet and pulled her against him with an arm banded low around her hips—not an embrace, she realized as every nerve inside her sang out in something a little too much like exultation, but so he could kick her jeans out from beneath her. And when he was done, her palms were flat against his gloriously bare chest and she could feel that great, scarred hand of his at the small of her back, and she thought she really might faint, after all.

"Can you not?" he asked her in that low, stirring voice of his, his head bent as if he was moments away from another one of those drugging, life-altering kisses that had ripped her whole world apart six months ago, so far apart even half a year on the run hadn't put it back together. "Are you certain?"

And she didn't mean to do it. She didn't know *why* she

did it. But she arched her back as if she couldn't help herself, and her breasts were so close then, so very close, to pressing against him the way she remembered they had that once, that delirious pressure that had undone her completely.

Kavian let out a small, indisputably male laugh then that did nothing at all to soothe her, and then, unaccountably, he let her go.

She stumbled back a step, and might actually have crumpled where she stood had that cool stone pillar not been right there behind her. She dug her fingertips in to it as if it were a life raft and still, her breath was as shallow as if she'd run a marathon or two.

"Take off the rest of your clothes, Amaya," Kavian said, and there was no mistaking the royal command. The powerful imperative. Or that surge of *something* inside her that wanted nothing more than to obey him. At once.

"I can't think of a single reason why I would do that." She managed to meet that gaze of his. Hold it. "More important, I don't want to take the rest—*any* of my clothes off."

"That is yet another lie. Soon there will be so many they will block out the desert sun above us, and I have no intention of living in such a darkness. Know this now."

That had the unpleasant ring of prophecy or foreboding, or perhaps more than a little of both, and it was as if her pulse had gotten too hard, too loud. It hammered at her.

"It's not a lie simply because it's something you don't want to hear," she threw at him, forcing her knees to lock beneath her, to stop their wobbling. "You don't own the thoughts in my head. You can't order me to think only the things you like."

His gray eyes gleamed, and there was not a single part of him that was not hard, unflinching. Tempered steel.

Barely contained power. She'd seen softer, more approachable statues littered about the sculpture gardens of Europe.

"It is a lie because you do, in fact, wish to take off the rest of your clothes." His voice was so quiet it almost disguised the cut of his words, the way they sliced into her. Through her. "More than that, you wish to give yourself over to me the way you did before, but this time, not in a sudden rush in a hidden alcove. You wish to run like honey against my palms and shake apart when I claim you. Again and again."

"No." But she scarcely made a sound.

"You are mine, Amaya. Can you doubt this? You shake even now, in anticipation."

"I was never yours. I will never be yours. I will—"

"Hush." An expression she might have called tender on another man, one not carved directly from stone and war and the cruel desert all around, crossed his brutally handsome face. He reached over and fit his hard palm to her jaw, cradling her too-hot cheek. "I did not know you were an innocent, Amaya. I would never have taken you like that, with so little consideration for anything but passion, had I known. You did not have to run, *azizty*. You could have told me."

And something yawned open inside her then. Something far more terrifying than the things he made her feel when he was autocratic and overbearing. She was drawn to him even then, yes. More than simply *drawn to him*. But this… She shoved the great sinkhole of it away in a panic, afraid it might spill out with that hectic heat she could suddenly feel behind her eyes. Afraid it marked her as weak and disposable, like her own mother before her.

Amaya jerked her cheek back, out of his hold, as if his palm had scalded her.

"I…" She felt too much, all at once, buffeting her from

all sides. Her memories and the present wound together into a great knot she couldn't begin to unravel—and was afraid to poke at, lest it fall apart and show him too much. She lied again, hoping it would push him back into temper, or put him off altogether. Anything but that hint of softness. *Anything but that.* "I wasn't innocent. I was the Whore of Montreal while I was at university. I slept with every man I could find in the whole of North America. I ran because I was bored—"

Kavian sighed. "And now I am bored."

She didn't know what he would do then and felt oddly bereft when he only stepped back from her. His dark gaze pinned her to the pillar behind her for a long, uncomfortably assessing moment that could easily have lasted whole years, and then he simply turned and dove into the nearest great bath.

It should have been a relief. A reprieve. She should have taken it as an opportunity to regroup, to breathe, to figure out what on earth she was going to do next as that solid, smooth warrior's body of his cut through the water and briefly disappeared beneath it.

But instead, she watched him. That marvelous, impossibly strong body could not possibly have been the product of a fleet of personal trainers or hours on modern gym equipment. He used every part of his intense physicality in everything he did. He was a smooth, powerful machine. And he fit here, in this age-old place. A weapon carved directly from the mountains themselves, beautiful and graceful in its way, but always, always deadly. Lethal in every particular.

Kavian surfaced in the middle of the pool and slicked his dark hair back from his face, his gaze like a punch, even from several feet away. Then he reached up with one perfectly carved arm and threw something toward the far end of the pool. It arced through the air and landed with a wet *splat*, and Amaya felt drunk. Altered. Because it still took another few moments to realize what he'd thrown was his boxer briefs.

And another jarring *thud* of her misbehaving heart to realize what that *meant*. That he was naked in all his considerable glory. Right there. Right in front of her.

She had to get a hold of herself, she thought sternly, or she was at definite risk of swallowing her own tongue and expiring on the spot. Which the Whore of Montreal would have been unlikely to do, surely.

"I don't understand what's happening," she said, forcing herself as close to an approximation of *calm* as she could get.

"Do you not? And yet you claimed you were no innocent. I'd have imagined that a woman of so much sordid experience would scarcely blink at the sight of a naked man in a pool."

He was no longer touching her. He was no longer caging her between his masterful body and that pillar. He was no longer even *near* her. So there was absolutely no reason that Amaya should have been standing there at the edge of the pool, staring at him as if he were holding her fast in one mighty fist.

"Is this—do you really want to—right here? You dragged me straight off the plane without any discussion or—"

He was pitiless. He said nothing, only watched her as she cut herself off and sputtered off into nothing as if she really were the artless, naive little girl he seemed to think she was already. She hated it. She hated herself. But she stood there anyway, as if awaiting his judgment. Or his next command.

As if it didn't matter what she felt, only what he did.

You know where that goes, she reminded herself with no little despair. *You know exactly where that leads, and who you'll become, too, if you let this happen.*

But all the vows she'd made to herself—that she would never lose herself so completely, that she would never disappear into any man until she could not exist without him the way her mother had done, until the loss of his affection sent her staggering around the planet like some kind of grieving gypsy with a thirst for vengeance and a child she resented—didn't seem to signify as she stood there in nothing but boy shorts and a T-shirt in the harem of the sheikh who had claimed her.

"This is a bath," Kavian said evenly. Eventually. Long after she was forced to come to several unfortunate conclusions about how very much she was like her mother, despite everything. "I dislike flying. I want the recycled air washed off my skin as soon as possible. And I want the last six months washed off you."

Amaya shivered, visibly, and Kavian tamped down the roaring beast in him that wanted nothing more than to put his hands on her and drag her to him, and who cared that she was anxious? He needed to be inside her. He needed her—and he had long since stopped *needing* a damn thing.

But he would not leap upon her like a feral thing, no matter the power of will it required to keep himself from doing so. This was no pretty diversion he was trying to lure into his bed for the night, not that he had ever needed much more of a lure than his name or his mere presence. Amaya was his queen. She would bear his sons, stand at his side, raise his heirs. She deserved what passed for a courtship here in this hard place he loved with every part of himself despite what he had done for it and no matter that there was only one possible, foregone conclusion.

This was a long game he played, with clear objectives. Like all the games he'd played in his time. And won.

So Kavian waited. He, who had not had to wait for much of anything since the day he reclaimed his father's throne. He, who had already waited for this woman for half a year, unaccountably. He, who was better used to women throwing themselves at him and begging for his notice.

He, who had never had a woman run from him in his life, before now. Before Amaya.

It was of little matter. She was here. She would stay here, because he willed it so. The world would return to the shape he preferred and do his bidding besides, and he would be inside her soon enough.

"Each pool is a different temperature," he said in the faintly bored tones of a tour guide, as if that fire in him didn't threaten to consume him whole despite the water he stood in. "There are any and all bathing accessories you could possibly require, from handmade soaps crafted here in the old city by local women to the finest luxury products flown in from Dubai."

She was beautiful even when she was obviously nervous, standing there in a small white T-shirt that she obviously wore nothing beneath and those stretchy little shorts that made her hips look nothing short of edible. Her legs were even longer than he'd imagined, and perfectly formed, giving her a bit more height than the average woman—which meant he would not dwarf her in bed or out. Her narrow feet were pale and delicate, and she'd painted her toes a cheerful, bright blue that made his chest feel tight and hit him as critically important, somehow. Though he knew that was foolish.

"Come in, Amaya," he said, invitation and order in one. "You will be the happier for it."

Her head canted slightly to one side. "Do you promise not to touch me?"

He let his gaze move over that full mouth of hers that he'd dreamed of, these past months, more than he cared to admit. That thick, dark hair he wanted to see swirling around her shoulders and that he wanted to feel slide across his own skin. Those small, proud breasts and the peaks he had yet to taste that he could see poking against the sheer fabric of her T-shirt, perhaps an invitation she didn't mean to extend. The hint of that smooth, olive expanse of her belly between her panties and her shirt, which he wanted to spend a very long time learning with his mouth. And that tempting triangle where her legs met, that he wanted to lick his way into until he forgot his own name.

Kavian took his time dragging his gaze back up her tempting body, noting the goose bumps that marked her arms as he did, and then smiled when his gaze tangled with hers again.

"No," he said. "I certainly do not."

Her lips parted as if that threw her off balance, but then she moved—and not away from him, as he'd expected. Instead, she walked along the edge of the pool toward the wide steps that led down into it from one side.

"Well," she said, with a certain primness that reminded him of that way she'd laughed at her brother in that long-ago video, and coursed through his veins like that same sweet wine. "I have nothing against hygiene, of course."

"Merely against sheikhs?" Perhaps, he thought with some surprise, he had it in him to tease after all. Only Amaya. Only alone.

"Sheikhs and kings and desert palaces," she agreed, her gaze touching his, then moving away again as she made her way down the wide stairs and on into the water, still wearing that shirt and those sexy little shorts as if they were some kind of swimming costume. "Awful things, I think we can all agree."

"Your misfortunes are vast, indeed. Of all the princesses I have chosen to become my queen over the course of my life, your burden is by far the heaviest."

Amaya moved farther into the water until it lapped at the sweet indentation of her waist, and skimmed her palms over the surface of the pool on either side of her, as if testing the water's temperature. She kept herself out of his reach, which Kavian could not abide a moment more. He moved toward her.

She watched him with as much enthusiasm as if he were an approaching shark. It shouldn't have been quite so entertaining, he supposed, but her various forms of defiance…delighted him. If that was what that sudden bright thing inside him was. He hardly recognized it.

"How many have there been?" she asked. When he didn't speak, when he only closed the distance between them, she swallowed in a way that belied that light tone she used. "Princesses that you've turned into queens? Am I the last in a long line? A parade?"

He didn't answer her. He liked the question too much, and what it told him of her, and she seemed to realize that. She danced back from him, then dropped abruptly, dunking her head beneath the water. For a moment she was a shimmer, the inky darkness of her hair obscuring her limbs from his view, and then she shot up again.

And the beast in him roared.

Her T-shirt was soaked through, showing him every contour of those glorious breasts, every mouthwatering detail. And better still, her hair had finally tumbled out of its braid and the dark mass of it coursed over her, framing her and presenting her like some kind of slick mermaid fantasy.

His mermaid fantasy, which Kavian hadn't realized he had until that moment.

She was swiping water from her face and she let out a sharp, high noise when she opened her eyes and found him there, much closer to her than he'd been when she submerged—which he also found entertaining.

He slid his hands over her hips, those sweetly rounded hips that had been seared into his memory, so deep that the tactile memories had kept him awake some nights. And then he pulled her toward him with his pulse a wild thunder in his veins, almost in pain, his need for her was so intense.

She gulped, but she didn't say a word, not even when he lowered his head and put his mouth *just there*, almost against her lips. *Almost.* He felt the fine tremors move through her, like an orchestra of *want*—a music that only she could hear. But Kavian could feel it. He felt the heat of her, let her scent—honey and rain—move in him like a blessing.

"I don't think I can kiss a man who kept seventeen women," she said, and he could feel each word against his mouth the same way he could feel the taut points of her nipples against his own chest, and neither was even close to enough. "I don't think I can reconcile myself to it, whether you emptied your harem or not."

"Then by all means, do not sully yourself," he said against the lush seduction of her mouth. "You can stand there and suffer. I do not mind at all."

And then he slid his hands up into the thick, wet glory of her hair, indulging himself. He dragged that smart mouth of hers the remaining millimeter toward his, and then finally, finally, he took her mouth with his.

CHAPTER FOUR

His kiss was like a bomb.

It detonated inside her, she burst into a shower of light and all the need and want and haunting desire that had been chasing her across the months she'd run from him slammed into her.

Amaya clung to him. She didn't think. She didn't *want* to think.

She kissed him back.

Just like six months ago, his kiss stormed through her. He wasn't gentle. He wasn't particularly kind. His kiss was carnal and dark, a blistering-hot invitation to a wickedness she'd experienced but once and still only vaguely understood.

But she wanted it. Oh, the things she *wanted* when this man took hold of her as if he had every right to her. As if her presence was all the surrender he required.

His hands moved from her hair to slide sleek against her skin, and she shuddered against him as he fit his hard palms to her breasts the same way he had done earlier to her cheek. But this was nothing like tender. This was pure, uncontainable wildness.

And it thrilled her, low and hot, dark and deep.

Amaya had never considered her breasts one way or the other. They were small, incapable of creating cleavage without help, and she'd have thought they weren't the least bit sensual or enticing. But that low growl in Kavian's throat, the one she felt inside her as he continued to take her mouth as if he truly did own her, made her think otherwise for the first time in her life.

Made her feel something like beautiful and cherished, all at once, which was as bright as another flame. And as dangerous.

When he pulled his mouth from hers, she let out a moaning noise she knew she'd later regret, which she almost regretted even as it happened—but in that moment, she didn't care. She couldn't.

There was that bright hot fire, dancing inside her. Whispering that she was as beautiful as he was, as powerful. Telling her that she was his. His mate, his match. *His*.

Amaya didn't even care when he let out that very male sound of laughter, of sheer and unmistakable victory. She felt the same thing shudder through her, as if the more he won this intimate battle of theirs, the more she did, too. She only shook when he pressed his open mouth to the column of her throat, and then she simply gave herself over into his talented hands.

The way she'd done once before. He made her mindless with longing. He made her shake with need.

He made her feel more alive, brighter and wilder and hotter and *right*, than she'd imagined was possible.

And Kavian knew exactly what he was doing. He bent his head to her breasts and this time he took one taut peak in his mouth. Then he lifted her against him with another matter-of-fact display of his superior strength, settling her so that she straddled his leg. The bright hot center of her was flush against the rock-hard steel of his thigh, and she could tell by the way that his hands moved to press her there that it was no accident.

And then he sucked her nipple in, deep and hard despite the T-shirt she wore, and the world disappeared.

Heat. Delight. That impossible blaze she'd half convinced herself she'd made up over all these long months alone and on the run—

He never removed her T-shirt, and that made the whole thing feel more illicit, more wild. Amaya could hardly breathe. Her thoughts crashed into each other and flew apart, and there was only him.

Only Kavian. Only this.

He toyed with her through the sheer material, using his hot mouth, the edge of his teeth, his remarkable hands, all the while keeping her in place against his hard thigh, where she couldn't help rocking herself with increasing intensity as the sensations stormed through her.

It was like being caught in a lightning storm, struck again and again and again.

Amaya couldn't imagine anyone could survive this— and she didn't care if she did. It was worth it, she thought. It was all worth it—

Harder and harder she moved herself against him, shameless and mindless at once, wanting only to *do something* about that wild need that shook through her and centered in her core. Wanting nothing more than *him*.

Kavian made a harsh noise, and that only lit her up all the brighter.

"You will be the death of me," he growled, low and intent, as if he read her mind.

As if, she managed to think with no little wonder, she had the same affect on this hard, wicked man as he did on her.

He took one nipple deep into the heat of his mouth again while his fingers rolled the other between them, lazy and sure. The twin assaults were like a new flash of light, a new storm. He did it once, then again, her core molten against his thigh.

"Now, Amaya," he ordered her, his mouth against her breast.

And Amaya shattered all around him, only aware that she screamed as she toppled straight over the edge into a wild oblivion when her own abandon echoed back from the walls as she lost herself completely in his arms.

When she came back to herself, Kavian had swept her up, high against his sculpted chest, and was carrying her out of the pool toward the central seating area. He wrapped her in a wide, soft bath sheet and sat her down on one of the lounging chairs. Amaya couldn't breathe—but then he left her there while he claimed his own bath sheet and tucked it around his lean waist, which only seemed to call more attention to the mouthwatering perfection of his glorious form.

She should say or do something, surely. She told herself she would, just as soon as her head stopped spinning. Or when he came back over here and claimed her once again, as he was surely about to do.

But he didn't.

Instead, Kavian went to the low table and the trays of food laid out for his pleasure. He took his time filling his plate with various local delicacies, and then sat in a lounge chair facing her where he could watch her as he ate.

Amaya didn't understand what was happening.

Her heart still pounded. She could feel it in her temples, her throat, her belly. And hot and soft between her legs.

"Aren't you going to…?"

She trailed off into nothing, irritated with herself. Why did this man turn her into the blushing, stammering fool she'd never been at any other point in her life? Why did he make her feel so foolish and so young with only the merest crook of his dark brow?

"If you cannot say it, Amaya, it does not exactly inspire me to do it," he replied mildly. Almost reprovingly, she thought.

And then he carried on eating, as if he hadn't left her in a spineless heap only moments before. As if that had all been a demonstration of some kind and he was entirely unaffected by the lesson he'd decided to teach her.

She didn't know why that made her furious, but it did—in a shocking, searing wave from her head all the way down to her feet. And if the rush of temper felt like some kind of relief, she told herself that hardly mattered. She struggled to sit up, ignoring the aftershocks of all that pleasure that still stampeded through her, as if he really had made her body his own.

She didn't want to think about that. She *refused* to think about that.

"I'm not a two-year-old," she threw at him instead. "I have no idea what your expectations are. We had sex once, by accident, and you chased me all over the planet for six months. You rant about how I'm *yours* and how I *gave myself to you.* But then you give me an orgasm and break for a quick snack. Right here in a subterranean bathhouse where you kept seventeen women under lock and key until recently, or so you claim. I have no idea what *reasonable* is under these circumstances. I have no idea what you're capable of doing." She pulled in a breath that felt much too ragged. "I don't have the slightest idea who you are."

That gaze of his took on an unholy gleam, but he only lounged back in his seat, looking otherwise unperturbed. Remote, as if she were looking at a carving on the side of a temple, not a man. She thought of ancient kings and actual thrones, feats of chivalry and strength and drawn-out, epic battles better suited to Tolkien novels, and found her throat was dry again.

"No one was held here under lock and key," he said after a moment, when she could feel anxiety like pinpricks all up and down her body, and was afraid she'd actually broken out in hives. "This is neither a prison nor a work of overwrought fiction."

"I'll keep that in mind the next time you start thundering on about promises."

Something far too dangerous to be amusement moved across that face of his and did not make her feel in the least bit secure. It occurred to her then that she was wearing nothing but a soaked-through T-shirt and panties, and a towel. And that this man had absolutely no qualm using her body against her when he felt like it.

But he didn't move toward her and prove that all over again, as she was far too aware he could. He stayed where he was, and Amaya couldn't understand how that was worse. Yet it was.

"And this might come as a great surprise to you," he said, his voice like smoke and temptation, "but thus far you are the only woman I have ever encountered who was not delighted at the prospect of sharing my bed."

"As far as you know, you mean." She glared at him, trying to be as furious with him as she should have been. Furious with herself that she was not. "People lie, especially to terrifying kings of the desert who threaten the very air they breathe."

"Ask yourself why I am so sure," he encouraged her, in a tone that made her stomach swoop toward the ground, though he could not have seemed more relaxed as he said it. No matter that glittering silver thing in his gaze. "Ask yourself how I can know this."

Amaya had absolutely no desire to do anything of the kind. Because she could think of several ways a man could be that certain, and he'd already demonstrated it to her twice. Six months ago in an alcove of the Bakrian Royal Palace and right here in the large pool today.

And she had no idea what must have showed on her face then, but Kavian only smiled, an edgy and dangerous crook of that hard, hard mouth of his she could still feel, as if he were still touching her when he was not.

That didn't help.

"You do not have to wonder about my expectations," he said, the way other men might comment on the weather. Their favorite sports team. Unlike with other men, whole armies he could command with a wave of his hand lurked beneath his words and settled around her neck like a heavy choke collar. "I do not traffic in subterfuge. I will tell you what I want. I will tell you how I want it and when. You will provide it, one way or another. It is simple."

"Nothing about that is simple." But he only gazed back at her, implacable and resolute, and she felt a searing kind of restlessness wash through her. Hectic. Almost an itch from deep within. She couldn't name it. But she couldn't sit still, either, and so she let it take her up and onto her feet. "I don't want to be here. I want to go home."

"If you wish it," he said amiably enough, and everything stopped. Her breath. Her heart. Had he truly agreed—and so easily? But that smile of his was not the least bit encouraging. It made her feel…edgy. *Edgier.* "Which home do you mean?"

Amaya thought in that moment that she might hate him. That she might never recover from it. That it was stamped deep into her bones, like a different kind of marrow, as much a part of her as her own.

It had to be hatred. It couldn't be anything else.

"You can return me to Canada," she bit out. "Right where you found me. I'll take it from there."

"Canada is not your home." Still he lounged there, as if this were a casual conversation. As if he weren't holding her between his hands like a giant, malicious cat, and toying with her because he could. Because he felt like it. Because he enjoyed using his damn claws. "You were born in Bakri. You lived there until you were eight years old. Then you and your mother wandered for the next decade. Here, there. Wherever the wind blew her, that is where you went. The longest you stayed anywhere in that time was fifteen months at a family-owned vineyard in the Marlborough wine region of New Zealand's South Island. Is that the home you mean? It pains me to tell you that the gentleman you stayed with then moved on from your mother's much-vaunted charms some time ago and now has a new family all his own."

Amaya remembered crisp mornings in a late New Zealand winter then, walking through the corridors of rich dirt and gnarled vines with the friendly man she'd imagined might make Elizaveta better. *Happier*, anyway—and he'd seemed to manage it, for a time. She remembered the long white-capped mountain range that stretched out lazily alongside her wherever she went, reaching from the vineyard she'd called home that year toward Blenheim and the sea in the east. The skittish sheep and curious lambs who marked her every move and bounded away from any signs of movement in their direction, real or imagined. The stout and orderly vineyards, set in their efficient lines all the way north to the foothills of the Richmond range.

Most of all she remembered the thick black, velvety nights, when the skies were so filled with stars they seemed messy, chaotic. Magic. Weighted down, as if, were she to blink, all that fanciful light might crush her straight down into the rich, fertile earth like nothing but another seedling. And yet somehow they'd made it impossible for Amaya to believe that she could really be as terribly alone as she'd sometimes felt.

She hadn't thought about that period of her life in a very long time. Elizaveta had moved on the way Elizaveta always did and Amaya had stopped imagining anyone could fix what her father had broken. She felt something crack inside her now, as if Kavian had knocked down a critical foundation with that unexpected swipe—but he was still talking. Still wrecking her with every lazily destructive word.

"Or perhaps you are referring to your years at university in Montreal?" He didn't wait for her to answer. "While it appeared to be a city you enjoyed, in many respects, you left it as often as possible during your studies. You went to the mountains, as we have established. But also to Europe. To the Caribbean for sun in the midst of all those relentless winters. And you left Canada altogether shortly after your graduation for Edinburgh, where you took up a very unsuitable job in a local pub while you made the most feeble of gestures toward a master's degree in some or other form of literature at the university there."

Amaya wanted to make a gesture toward him that was anything but feeble, but restrained herself. Barely. She felt the prick of her own nails against her palms, and wished she could sink them into him instead.

"It's not up to you to decide what feels like home to me. My life is not something that requires your input or critique." She fought to keep her voice even. "You can tell because I didn't ask you for either one."

"Unfortunately for you, it is indeed up to me." Kavian shrugged, and it was not a gesture of uncertainty on a man like him. It was another weapon, and Kavian, she was beginning to understand all too well, did not hesitate to use the weapons he had at his disposal. "You do not have a home, Amaya. You never have. But that, too, has changed now. Whether you are prepared to accept that or not is immaterial."

She couldn't breathe. She felt as if he'd thrown her down a staircase, as if she'd landed hard on her back and knocked all the air from her lungs, and for a moment she could do nothing but stare back at him.

"I want to be somewhere you are not," she managed to grate out, finally.

"I am sure you do. But that is not among the choices available to you."

"This is a huge palace. There has to be a room somewhere you can stash me, far away from everything and everyone. I don't care if it's a dungeon, as long as it's nowhere near you."

Where she could figure out how to breathe through this, recover from this. If that was even possible.

Where she could work out what the hell she was going to *do*.

"There are many such rooms, but you will be staying in mine."

He only watched her, utterly without mercy. And she didn't know which was worse, the wet heat threatening to spill from her eyes, the simmering flame deep in her core that she wanted to deny, the shaking she couldn't quite seem to control now he'd upended the whole of her life in a few short sentences or the fact that he'd trapped her here. In every possible way, and they both knew it.

"No," she said.

But it was as if she hadn't spoken. It made her wonder if she had.

"I apologize if this distresses you, but I am not a particularly modern man," Kavian replied. He did not sound remotely apologetic. Nor did he look it. "I do not trust what I cannot touch. I want you in my bed."

Bed. The word exploded inside her, ripping through her with a trail of white-hot images that centered on his mouth, his hands, that body of his above her and around her and in her—

"I don't want to be anywhere near your bed. You've already done as you like with me in an alcove, a pool—why can't we leave it at that?" She sounded hysterical. She felt hysterical. "Why can't we just *leave it*?"

Kavian, by contrast, went very, very still, though his dark eyes burned.

And she felt another foundation crumble into dust at that look on his face.

"The next time I take you, Amaya, two things will happen," he said softly. So very softly. It was a whisper that rolled through like a battle cry. "First, it will be in a proper bed. I may not be civilized, precisely, but I do have my moments. And I wish to take my time. All the time in the world, if necessary." He waited for her to shudder at that, as if he'd expected it. Then he nearly smiled again, which was its own devastation. "And second, you will use my name."

"Your name?"

"You have yet to utter it," he pointed out, and she could see that though he still lounged there, though his voice was almost as languid as he looked, there was absolutely nothing *mild* about him at all. That *mildness* was an illusion he used to do his bidding, nothing more, like everything else. "I assume this is yet another attempt on your part to maintain distance between us. Is it not?"

"I have no idea what you're talking about. I say your name all the time, usually as a curse word."

"You will use my name." He didn't rise. He didn't have

to. It was as if he held her tight between those hands of his even as he reclined in his chair. She was sure she felt the press of his palms, like all those New Zealand stars when she'd been thirteen, crushing her deep into the earth. "You will sleep in my bed. You will give yourself to me. There will be no distance between us, Amaya. There will be nothing but my will and your surrender."

"Followed by my suicide, as quickly as possible, to escape you," she threw back at him to hide the pounding of her heart that told her truths she didn't want to face.

But Kavian only laughed at her, as if he could hear it. As if he knew.

CHAPTER FIVE

AMAYA HADN'T MEANT to fall asleep.

The smiling, almost too deferential attendants had been waiting for her when she'd pushed her way out of the baths, still reeling from all that had happened with Kavian. They'd surrounded her as they'd led her through the gleaming labyrinth of a palace, and Amaya hadn't been able to tell if they were deliberately taking her on a confusing route to her rooms or if the palace really was that difficult to navigate.

Either way, they'd deposited her in a rambling suite of rooms that clearly belonged to the king himself. And had pretended they didn't understand her when she demanded to be taken elsewhere.

"I don't want to stay here," she'd told them, again and again, until she'd finally had to take it up with the two intimidatingly ferocious guards who stood at the doors.

They'd only stared back at her, without any of the sweet smiles or pleasing laughter of her attendants.

"I need my own rooms," she'd said stubbornly. "This is a mistake. I'm not staying here."

The guards had only stared back at her, for what had seemed like an inordinate amount of time, especially when Amaya realized she was wearing nothing but the robe the attendants had wrapped her in.

"You may take that up with the king if you feel it is your place to question him," the larger of the two guards replied eventually, in a tone that suggested this conversation was itself scandalous and inappropriate—or perhaps, Amaya had realized belatedly, it was simply that *she* was. After all, from this man's perspective, she wasn't the unfairly trapped woman who deserved to make her own choices in life no matter whose blood ran in her veins—she was the princess who had been exalted by his beloved king's notice only to throw her good fortune in the sheikh's face by running away.

She'd been certain she could *see* that very sentence run through the man's expression like a tabloid ticker at the bottom of a television screen. That—and the fact that he and his compatriot looked as if they'd have relished the opportunity to chase her down in the corridor like an errant fox—made her retreat into the suite and shut the door.

Amaya had stood there for a long moment, breathing much harder than she should have been, her back against the door that represented her only path out of Kavian's rooms, her bare feet cold against the chilly marble floor of the sheikh's grand foyer.

That was when she'd decided that her best bet wasn't to run. That should have been obvious. He'd already caught her once, in the most remote place she'd known. Her only option now was to hide.

Surely Kavian couldn't be *that much* a barbarian, she'd told herself stoutly as she wandered from room to room in the rambling collection of gorgeous chambers on two floors that composed His Majesty's royal suite. There were two or three elegant salons, making clever use of the many stacked terraces and the sweeping views down into the hidden, protected valley. The marble foyer opened into a private courtyard with a graceful fountain claiming its center.

Several sitting rooms were scattered here and there along with a media center, a well-stocked library, even a formal dining room dressed in silk tapestries and golds.

She'd kept looking for a hiding place. Kavian might have talked a big game there by the bathing pools, but the reality was that he'd never forced her to do anything, as shameful as that might have been to admit. The truth was that she'd agreed to marry him in some pathetic attempt to please her brother and possibly her dead father, and then she'd melted all over Kavian every time he touched her.

Amaya didn't fear him physically. She feared herself. She feared the depth of her own surrender and how much a part of her wanted nothing more than to sink to her knees and exult in Kavian's claim over her. To let him keep every one of those dark, delicious promises he'd made to her. To learn precisely what he meant when he told her she would learn *obedience*…

Stop it, she'd snapped at herself as she moved from room to room. She was a liberated woman, damn it. She might have been born into a society like this one, she might even have been briefly nostalgic enough to let her brother talk her into returning to it after their father's death a few years back, but her heart wasn't here. Her heart had never been here.

It can't be here, she'd assured herself. Because she'd seen what leaving a heart behind in a harsh place like this could do to a woman, hadn't she? She'd spent her entire childhood handling the aftermath of her ever more brittle mother's broken heart.

But that particular organ was all too traitorous, she'd realized then, when she walked into a gilt-edged room that Kavian clearly used as a private office and saw the portrait of the man himself hanging there on the wall, in thick oils and bold shades that made him seem a part of the very desert he commanded. And her heart had thumped at her. Hard.

Too hard, as if it had its own agenda.

She'd rubbed at her chest, annoyed that the attendants had taken her clothes from her and given her nothing to wear but a silky thing she refused to acknowledge was some kind of negligee and a raw-silk wrapper to ward off the complete lack of chill in the air. She might as well have been laid out on a silver platter, trussed and bound for Kavian's pleasure—

That was not a calming image. She'd shoved it out of her head, but not before her entire body had broken out in goose bumps. *Damn him.*

She'd finally settled on Kavian's dressing room. It was a vast space, much larger than the dormitory rooms she'd lived in while in halls at university and probably bigger than the whole of the flat she'd shared with three other postgraduates during her brief time in Edinburgh. She'd ignored the rows of exquisitely cut suits that had clearly been made in the finest couture houses for Kavian alone, the traditional robes in the softest and most gorgeous of fabrics that she couldn't help touching as she passed, all the trappings of a great man who could dress to kill in any scenario he chose.

She'd ignored the somersaults her heart and belly did at the sight of all that sartorial splendor that summoned him to her mind as if he'd stood there before her, those slate-gray eyes gleaming silvery and lethal.

And then she'd crawled into the farthest, darkest corner and curled up amid a selection of what appeared to be stout winter boots and dark wool overcoats, hiding herself from view.

She'd meant to wait him out. To see what he'd do when

he returned to the suite—as he'd do soon, she had no doubt, because she'd been quite certain he'd meant every word he said to her near the bathing pools—and if maybe, just maybe, the fact that she'd been moved enough to hide from him would impress her position on him with far more emphasis than mere words.

But she hadn't planned to fall asleep.

She jolted awake with a terrific start, but for a panicked moment she couldn't figure out what was happening. Kavian loomed above her, and the world spun drunkenly and by the time Amaya understood what was going on, he'd hauled her out of her hiding place and into his arms.

"You have the mark of my boot upon your face," he said, his voice cool and yet with all that power of his seething beneath it, like the darkest shadows. "How very dignified you are, my queen."

Amaya would have said she wasn't particularly vain, that there'd been no point with a mother like Elizaveta, who had been a model in her youth, and yet her hand moved to her cheek anyway. It felt nothing but hot, and the way he gazed at her while he held her against that steel-hard chest of his didn't help.

"It should tell you something that I'm willing to go to such lengths to avoid you," she said, hating the rasp of sleep in her voice. She tried to pull herself together despite the fact that he'd started to move—but every step he took made her far too *aware*.

Of him. His strength. His heat. The hardness of his chest, the granite bands of his arms around her. And of herself, too. The way the silk moved over her skin. The lick of flame that followed every soft, sleek shift of the fabric against her belly, her hips, her breasts.

"It tells me a great many things," he agreed, in what did not sound like a particularly sympathetic tone of voice.

He shifted her, which had the cascading effect she most wanted to avoid, a spinning sort of caress that sank deep into her core and was nothing short of a full-body betrayal. She sucked in a breath audibly. He glanced down at her as he moved through the door, out of his dressing room and into the larger sitting area that lay between it and the actual bedroom she hadn't wanted to investigate too closely earlier.

She could see sunlight on the far side of the sitting room, drowning the terrace that ran the length of it in all that golden desert light, and she couldn't have said why that made her breath catch. As if she'd imagined he could only come after her in the dark? But she'd known better, surely. Kavian didn't play by any rules. Ever.

But she kept trying to make him. What other choice did she have?

"Does it tell you that you are a monster?" She knew it was dangerous to poke at him when he was holding her like this, when there was no possibility of escape. But she couldn't seem to stop herself. "That you are so overwhelming and so unreasonable that I was forced to hide in a closet to try to get through to you?"

"That," Kavian said. "And the fact that you are desperate. I suspect you think that if you act like a child, I might be tempted to treat you like one instead of the woman we both know you are."

There was no reason that should have stung. "I've never claimed I was a child."

"That is wise, Amaya, as the definition of a *child* is markedly different in my country. We, for example, do not coddle our young well into their twenties, then welcome them into our homes again until such a time as they feel sufficiently inspired to begin an adult life. We expect them to assume their duties far younger, and then take responsibility for the choices they've made. I myself was a soldier at thirteen and something far less palatable when I was barely twenty. I was never treated like a boy."

"If you think either one of my parents coddled me in any way, at any point in my life, you're insane."

She hadn't meant to say that, certainly, and could have bitten her tongue once she did. Kavian only gazed down at her for a brief, electric instant—but that glimmering moment of contact seared through her.

"I know exactly who and what you are," he said as he strode through the far door into his bedchamber, a stately affair in dark woods and richly masculine shades of red and gold. "Whether you stage melodramatic displays in my closet or race across the planet in a bid to humiliate me in front of the world, it is all the same to me. It will all end right here."

And then he set her down on his bed.

As punctuation.

Amaya expected him to leap on her, but of course he didn't do that. He simply stood there before her, a part of the magnificence of the room, the palace—and at the same time its intensely masculine focal point. He'd donned a pair of very loose white trousers that flowed around him and somehow made him look even more like the desert king he was than anything else she'd ever seen him in. And that was it. He folded his arms over the golden expanse of that carved and battered chest of his that shouldn't have been half so appealing, and watched her.

And she wanted to run. In her head, she threw herself to the side, she scrambled across the slippery gold coverlet and leaped from the mattress, she threw herself off the side of the terrace into thin air to escape him—

But in reality, she did none of those things. She was frozen into place. She was too tense and she couldn't quite breathe and she *hurt*... Except she realized, one shuddering, shallow breath after the next, that it was a very specific kind of ache, located in a very particular place.

And worse, that the knowing expression on his hard face and that silvery awareness in his gaze meant he knew it.

How could he know it? But he did.

"You didn't have to chase me." Amaya hardly knew what she was saying. "You could have let me go."

His hard mouth flirted with the possibility of a curve. But then didn't give in to it.

"Are you wet?" he asked.

For a moment, Amaya didn't understand. The baths had been hours ago and she'd dried off with the towel—

Then she got his meaning, and she simply *ignited.*

The flush lit her up, inside and out. She was certain she was bright red, searing and glowing, *neon*, and she could neither pull a full breath into her lungs nor look away from him. Much less control the surge of desire that pooled between her legs.

"I will take that as a yes," he said, sounding darkly amused and something far more dangerous besides. "You already came apart in my hands today, Amaya. Do you doubt that you are mine? I wasn't even inside you."

She should have leaped to her feet then. Slapped him. Screamed at him. Made it clear to him that this kind of behavior was completely unacceptable—that he couldn't treat her like this. That she wouldn't *let* him.

But Amaya did none of those things. She only stared back at him, that ache in her growing hotter and more desperate by the moment.

"I want you naked," he said, and there was a certain gruffness to his voice then. A certain edge that told her that perhaps he wasn't as unaffected by this as he was pretending he was.

"I don't want—"

"Now, Amaya." That gruffness turned to granite and pounded through her veins. "I already stripped you once today. Don't make me do it again." His gaze moved over her face, and she was sure there was something wrong with her, that she should feel it like a caress. That she should long for more. "Show me, *azizty*. Show me you are as proud of your beauty as I am."

Something shifted deep inside her, then turned over. It was like a dream, she told herself. And the truth was, she'd had this dream. Again and again. This, or something like this, all across the long months since she'd fled the Bakrian Royal Palace on the night of their betrothal. It always starred Kavian in some or other state of undress, so that part was familiar, though he was far more magnificent in reality. And it always involved this same roller-coaster sensation inside her, hot and then cold, high and then low, a longing and an ache and a *need*.

This is just another dream, she assured herself.

And in a dream nothing she did mattered, so she could do as she liked in the moment. It had no meaning. It held no greater significance. She could lose herself in that calm, ruthlessly patient gray gaze of his as if it was a way home. She could let that become what mattered instead.

So that was what she did.

Amaya pulled the wrapper off her, letting it slide over the skin it bared, in an almost unconscious sensual show. Then, before she could question her motives, she pulled the silken little scrap she wore beneath it up and over her head, tossing it with the wrapper so they sat there in a slippery heap of deep blue against the gold coverlet.

Then she swallowed, hard, and simply sat there.

Completely naked, as he'd commanded.

And she knew that it didn't mean anything. That it was

nothing more than a psychological trick to imagine it was the crossing of a very serious line. She'd lost her virginity to this man in a shocking rush six months ago. He'd had his mouth and his hands on her in the palace pools only today. But both of those times, she'd had clothes on.

It was amazing how different it was to sit before him, utterly naked, for the very first time.

"Why are your shoulders rounded like an ashamed teenager's?" he asked her, so mildly that she'd have thought that he hadn't noticed her nudity at all were it not for that near-hectic glitter in his gaze. "Why are you slumped before me as if you do not know your worth? Is this how you offer yourself to me, Amaya? In apology?"

"I'm not apologizing." She didn't think she was offering herself to him, either, so much as following his orders for reasons she didn't care to examine too closely—but somehow that part got tangled on her tongue and stayed in her mouth.

"Are you certain? I have seen more tempting sea turtles, tucked away in their shells where no one can see them." As if he'd said that purely to make her flush with temper, his mouth curved slightly when she did. "Sit up. Arch your back as if you are proud of your breasts."

"I think we both know perfectly well that they're nothing to be proud of. Why flaunt what I don't have?"

"I am not interested in your opinion of them." His eyebrows edged higher on his forehead, as if he was amazed at her temerity. "I am recalling how they felt in my mouth. More, please."

She hadn't realized that she'd done as he asked until then. But she had. She'd sat up and let her back arch invitingly. That presented her breasts to him, yes, and it also made her hair move around her shoulders, and she knew, somehow, that he liked that, too.

And for a long moment—it could have been years, for all she knew—he simply looked at her.

It should have been boring. She should have felt awkward. Exposed. Embarrassed. Cold, even.

But instead, Amaya burned. She ached. She *wanted*.

"Look at you," Kavian said softly. "Your breath comes faster and faster. You are flushed. If I were to reach between your thighs, what would I find?"

She couldn't answer him.

"It would take so little," he continued, his voice almost soft. "Your nipples are so hard, aren't they? Think of all the things I could do with them. Think how it would feel." She shifted against the bed beneath her, pressing herself against it and hardly aware of what she was doing, and he laughed. "None of that. You will come for me or not at all, Amaya. Remember that, if you please."

She knew, distantly, that there were a hundred things she should say. She should challenge him. She should fight him. She should refuse to act like this simply because he wanted her to do it—but she knew, of course she knew, that he wasn't the only one who wanted it. And she wasn't sure she could face what that said about her, what it made her.

So perhaps it was easier to simply do as he asked instead.

"Kneel up," he told her in that same low, knowing voice, as if he was already inside her. As if he was in her mind, as well. As if he knew all those dark, twisted things she couldn't admit to herself. "Right where you are."

"I'm not going to kneel before you and beg you for— for anything," she threw at him. But she didn't sound like herself and he didn't look particularly moved by her outburst.

"Of course not. You are so appalled by all of this, I am sure."

"I am."

"I can see that." His head canted slightly to one side, and those slate-gray eyes gleamed silver. "Kneel up, Amaya. Do not make me ask you again."

This, right here, was the moment of truth. She didn't entirely comprehend why she'd taken her clothes off when he told her to, but she couldn't unring that bell. But this, here, *now*—this was where she had to draw the line.

It was simple. All she needed to do was stand up. Climb off this bed and walk away. Kavian was many things, but she didn't believe he was truly a brute. Hard, yes. The hardest man she'd ever met. But she understood on some deep feminine level of intuition she hadn't known she possessed that while he might merrily shove away at her boundaries, he wouldn't actually force her into anything. All she needed to do was get off this bed.

She moved then, though her body hardly felt like hers. She could feel every part of her skin, as if every square inch of it was alive in a way it never had been before—a way *she* never had been until now. She felt so highly sensitive it was as if the air around them were a thick, padded thing, massaging her.

Maybe that was why she didn't really notice what she was doing until she'd already done it. And then she was kneeling there before him, precisely as he'd commanded her to do.

That was bad enough. Worse, when he only looked at her, she arched her back again, pulling her shoulders back and presenting him with her breasts as he'd asked her to do before. Not only her breasts—her whole body. Right there before him.

This *was* the silver platter, she understood then. She'd climbed up onto it and undressed for it and arranged herself on it, all for him.

Her pulse skittered through her body, wild and erratic and much too fast.

He waited.

She didn't know how she knew he was waiting, but she did. He was.

And the air between them seemed charged. Spiked. She couldn't see anything but that hard, oddly patient gaze of his. She couldn't *feel* anything but hunger. A deep, dark, consuming hunger that made her knees feel so weak she was deeply, wildly grateful that she wasn't trying to stand.

She wanted him to touch her. She wanted him to take her the way he had done that night six months ago, the way he had today in that pool. She wanted *him*.

"Then you must say the word, *azizty*, and you will have me," he murmured, and Amaya realized to her horror that she'd said all of that out loud.

Her throat was as dry as if she'd inhaled the whole of the desert outside. She shook, over and over, and she didn't think she'd stop. She understood that this was a line she could never uncross. That there would be no returning to who she'd been before. That if she was honest, it had already happened six months ago and she'd simply been trying her best to deny it all this time. Running and running and ending up right back where she'd started.

Worse, this time, because she knew not only what she was doing, but what he could do, too.

"Please," she whispered. But that wasn't what he was looking for.

"Say it," he ordered her, his voice tight.

She didn't pretend it wasn't a full and total surrender. But in that moment, she wasn't sure she cared.

You will use my name, he'd told her. Perhaps the begging part had been implied, even then.

Amaya didn't care about that, either.

"Please," she said again. "Kavian, *please*."

Kavian smiled. It was very male. Dark and satisfied. It made her whole body light up and burst into flame.

And then he reached for her and made it all that much worse.

CHAPTER SIX

KAVIAN WANTED TO throw her down and sink deep inside her in that instant. He wanted to slake the white-hot burn of *hunger* inside him, made all the worse for the uncharacteristic restraint he'd showed these past months while he scoured the planet for her.

He'd found to his great surprise that after he'd had Amaya, even in such a blind rush, no other woman would do.

She would pay for that, too.

But first he would bind her to him in a way she'd never untangle. First, he would make certain she saw nothing else in all the world but him. He would make her need him more than air and maybe then she would stop looking for exit strategies. He wanted to own her, body and soul. But first, he would worship her.

Kavian told himself they were the same thing.

And if the idea of having her completely at his command—the way she should have been since the day of their betrothal—made that tight thing in his chest feel easier, well, he told himself it was the conquest that fired his blood, nothing more. That tightness was about the injustice and sheer insult of the way she'd kept herself from him, that was all. She was his. It was time she behaved as if she knew that at last, as if she finally understood her place.

Because Kavian was king of this harsh land, not a bloodhound who could roam the earth forever in search of his runaway bride. He had won back his father's throne with his blood, his strength. He ruled Daar Talaas with his own cunning and his commitment to defend what was his no matter the cost. He'd had no choice but to chase down the woman who had tried to shame him in the eyes of his people.

More than that, he'd wanted her. He thought he would always want her. *She was his.*

But it was past time he got back to the intricate business of running this ancient, desert-hardened place, or he would lose it to someone who would do so in his stead. That was the law of Daar Talaas. That was the price of power—it belonged only to the man who could wield it.

His relationship with this woman could be no different. He would not allow it.

Kavian took Amaya's sweetly rounded chin in his hand and held her there, though he knew he could hold her as easily with his gaze. He could feel the way she shivered at his touch. He could see emotion and longing in those dark eyes of hers, and he reveled in both. He could smell the delicate scent of her soft skin and the sweet fragrance that rose from the masses of her dark hair she finally wore down around her pretty shoulders.

And beneath it all rose the far richer fragrance of her arousal.

The only thing he'd ever wanted more, in all his life, was the throne he'd won back through his own fierce determination. He'd found the darkness within him; he'd become it. He'd used it to do what was necessary. He'd been raised on vengeance and he'd finally taken his when he was barely twenty. And even that—the achievement of his life—seemed far off just now, with Amaya naked and obedient before him, her gaze fixed to his.

This is the way back to reality, he assured himself. *Conquer her here, now, and you will never need to risk the throne for her again.*

He'd known that he wanted Amaya from the moment he saw that video of her. And he'd known precisely how he would take her, and how she would thrill to it, the moment he met her in her brother's palace. He'd suspected then that she would fit him perfectly.

Now he knew it as well as he knew his own name.

Six months ago, the wild passion between them had been a burst of flame, unexpected and all consuming. They'd met for the first time when Kavian arrived with his entourage at the Bakrian Royal Palace to claim her as his betrothed and begin the official alliance between their two countries. It had been a formal and very public greeting of political allies, an elegant affair in a majestic salon, surrounded on all sides by ministers and aides, ambassadors and carefully selected palace reporters who could be relied upon to trumpet the appropriate information into all the correct ears.

There had been all those contracts to sign, all those oaths to take, and this woman he'd agreed to marry had been dressed in a fine, formal gown that made her look every inch the untouchable desert princess. They'd talked with excruciating politeness while surrounded and closely observed on all sides. They'd been feted at a long, formal dinner ripe with too many speeches from what seemed like every Bakrian noble in the whole of the kingdom. And for all that they'd sat next to each other during the endless evening, they'd never been out of that too-public fishbowl for even a moment. There had been no real conversation, no chance of anything but the loosest connection.

Then they'd had their betrothal ceremony the following day, in the grand ballroom of the palace that had been draped in every shade of gold in the glare of too many cameras to count. Cameras and gossips and a parade of aristocrats to comment on every last bit of it. Like carrion crows, pecking away at them.

"In my country," Kavian had told her as they'd made their formal entrance together, touching only in that stiffly appropriate manner that befitted their respective ranks on such an occasion and before so many judgmental eyes, "there is no need for a wedding ceremony. It is the claiming that matters, not the legalities that follow. A wedding is all but redundant."

"My brother's kingdom may not sit at the forefront of the modern age, exactly," Amaya had replied, and he'd been lost in the bittersweet chocolate gleam in her eyes, the sweet lushness of her lips, that kick of deep, dark need that had haunted him since the moment he saw her face. To say nothing of the unscripted, less than perfectly polite thing she was saying then and that flashed in her gaze, giving him a hint of the woman beneath the high-gloss Bakrian princess adorning his arm. A glimpse of that defiance of hers that sang to him. "But he does prefer that any royal marriages be legalized. As do I, I will admit."

"As you wish," Kavian had murmured. In that moment, he'd thought he'd give her anything she asked for another glimpse beneath her surface. His name, his protection, that went without saying. His kingdom, his wealth, his lands, certainly. His blood. His flesh. His life. Whatever she desired.

But she'd kept her gaze trained on the ceremony, not on him.

He'd hated it.

They'd exchanged their initial vows, there before the kings of the surrounding realms, sheikhs and rulers and sultans galore. Officials and ministers, the ranks of Bakrian aristocrats and the high-placed members of his own cabinet. Her brother. His men.

And then, once it had been finished and all the rest of the formal speeches about unity and family had been made for the benefit of their enemies in the region, Kavian took his betrothed aside so they could finally, *finally*, have a moment to themselves.

Merely a moment, he'd thought. He hadn't had anything planned. He'd only wanted a little bit of privacy with her, with no eyes on them and nothing but their real faces. He'd wanted to see what was between them then, when there was no one but the two of them to judge it, pick over it, analyze it.

He had congratulated himself on his magnanimity, proud of himself that he was not like his own forefathers, that he had every intention of winning this woman slowly and carefully—instead of throwing her over his saddle and riding off into the desert with her like the Bedouin chiefs of old who made up a sizable portion of his family tree. He'd had absolutely no intention of playing the barbarian king to a deeply Westernized woman like Amaya, who no doubt had all sorts of opinions about what *civilized* meant. Oh, no. He'd planned to wine her and dine her like all the urbane sophisticates he'd imagined she'd known all her life, in all the cities she'd visited in all those concrete and glass places he abhorred. He'd planned to do what he had to do, whatever it took, to bind her to him in every way.

She'd led them to that alcove, tucked away out of sight in a far-off corner of the ballroom's second-floor balcony while the rest of the assembled throng moved about far below, reveling in Rihad al Bakri's lavish hospitality. Kavian had stared down at her when they were finally alone.

He hadn't smiled. He'd been trying to see inside her, trying to match her exquisite beauty in person to the image he'd carried around with him in his head. He'd been trying to process the fact that she was well and truly his already, no matter *how* he approached her.

It had felt like sunlight, deep inside him, warm and bright. He hadn't known what to make of it.

"Well," she'd said with false brightness. "Here we are. Officially betrothed and still total strangers."

"We are not strangers," he'd corrected her, with far more gruffness than he'd intended. He hadn't meant to speak. He'd found those intricate braids that she'd worn like a crown of her own glossy hair an enchantment, and he'd been deep in their spell. He'd felt her gaze like a caress, an incantation. "I will soon be your husband. You are already mine."

"I'm not yours yet," she'd said, and then she'd lifted her chin in a kind of challenge that he'd only understood, in retrospect, had been a bit of foreshadowing he should have heeded. Back then, he'd simply enjoyed it. "And you should know that I can't marry a man with a harem. A betrothal for political purposes is one thing, especially if it helps my brother, but a marriage under such circumstances? No. I refuse."

Kavian had only continued to watch her, as if it was a deep thirst he felt and she the only possibility of ever quenching it. Most people caved under his regard, and quickly. Amaya had only squared her shoulders and held his gaze.

He'd liked that. Far too much, truth be told.

"For you," he'd said, as if she had any choices left, as if she hadn't just signed herself over to his keeping in full view of two countries and by now, the better part of the world, "I will empty mine. Is that what you require? Consider it done."

He'd stopped restraining himself then. He'd looked at her with all that fire, all that dark longing, right there on the surface. He hadn't hidden a single bit of the beast inside him. He hadn't tried.

And Amaya had done the most extraordinary thing. She'd flushed, hot and red and flustered—but not frightened. Not horrified. Not even particularly scandalized— all of which he'd expected, on some level. Just...*hot*. Then she'd looked away as if the heat was too much. As if *this* was too much. As if he was.

As if she felt exactly as he did.

Everything in him had roared, approval and acknowledgment.

Mine, he'd thought, with every cell in his body. With every breath.

And he'd taken her head between his hands, those braids warm and soft beneath his palms, and he'd tasted her for the first time. It had changed everything.

It had blown them both up, right then and there.

That flame had only intensified in all the months since, while he'd had nothing to do while he chased her but imagine her right here, naked before him in his very own bed, the way she was right now. *Finally.*

"Why are you staring at me like that?" Amaya asked, and he could hear the nerves in her voice. The hunger and the heat.

He'd been right about her—about this magnificent chemistry between them—six months ago. He was right now, too.

"I keep telling myself I am going to take this slow," he said, dropping his hand from her chin but moving closer to her. "Act like the sophisticated gentleman I am not. But that is unlikely, *azizty*. Very, very unlikely, the longer you look at me with those big, innocent eyes of yours that are nothing but a temptation."

"My eyes aren't innocent." It was as if she couldn't help herself, when she must know he knew she lied. "They're wicked. As dirty and debauched as the rest of me. I keep trying to tell you."

He only gazed back at her until he saw that flush again, warming her skin, prickling over all the soft flesh on display before him. Just as he recalled it. Then he smiled. Slightly.

"I want you to take it slow," she whispered.

"No," he said, gathering her into his arms and pulling her against the wall of his chest, exulting in the way she slid against him, then melted into him, as if she really had been made to his precise specifications. "You do not."

And then he settled his mouth over hers, at last, and let the fire break free, searing both of them.

Kavian *consumed* her.

There was no other word for it.

His kiss was a slick addiction. A wild, impossible ride, and she couldn't get enough. He held her against him and he angled her head where he wanted it and he simply *feasted*.

And Amaya loved it.

The more he took, the more she gave, meeting every slide of his tongue against hers. She arched into him, pressing her aching breasts against the dizzying wonder of his hard chest, reveling in the sensation of that strong hand of his on her bottom, kneading her. Guiding her.

Driving her crazy with need.

He pulled his mouth away from hers, letting out a very

male sound of satisfaction at the small, disappointed noise she couldn't keep herself from making.

"Be patient, *azizty*," he said in that dark way of his, and she didn't know how she knew that he was teasing her. That he was deliberately drawing this out to make that ache in her intensify.

Or that he would continue to do it until he felt like stopping; that what she wanted would have nothing to do with it.

She loved that, too. She had the sense he'd known she would.

Kavian took his time, lazily tracing a path down her neck to taste every inch of her collarbone. Then he dropped his head to play with her breasts again, making her moan and shake against him as he tested the plumpness of each of them, then tasted and tugged each proud peak.

This time, he didn't let her topple over that edge. This time, he had more on his agenda. He swept her up and then he laid her out on that big, wide bed, stretched himself out beside her, and kept going.

He licked his way over her navel, then lower, laughing as she bucked against him, lost somewhere between desire and delirium, and she didn't much care which as long as he kept touching her. Tasting her. Making her feel more beautiful, more precious, than she'd had any idea she could feel.

"Kavian." She didn't mean to say his name. She hardly knew what she was doing as he took her hips in his big hands and held her there before him as if she truly were a feast and he was nothing but hungry. "Please."

"I like that," he said approvingly, and she could *feel* his voice against that most private part of her that was molten and aching and already his. It made her shudder, deep within, the feeling radiating out everywhere, coursing in her veins and washing over her whole body. "Beg me."

And then he licked his way straight into the core of her.

Amaya exploded.

She thought she screamed his name, or maybe that was only what it *felt* like inside her, and either way she was lost in the storm of sensation. Lost completely. It swept her away. It altered her very being.

It was like dying, and the crazy part was how much she loved it. All of it.

She felt like someone else entirely when she came back to that bed with a jolt and found Kavian propped up above her and entirely naked, holding his weight on his elbows while the hardest part of him probed at her entrance.

He looked harsh. Unsmiling, as ever. And incredibly, impossibly beautiful.

Amaya couldn't seem to breathe. She was falling, she realized—tipped off the side of the world and tumbling end over end without any hope of stopping, washed out to sea forever in that dark gray gaze of his.

He looked at her as if he wanted to eat her alive. He looked at her as if he already had done so.

She wanted to say a thousand things. She wanted to tell him of that mess inside her that was all his doing, that she hadn't known could exist. She *wanted*, and yet she couldn't seem to do it. Instead, she held that terrible and wonderful gaze of his, and she only reached up and slid her hand along his proud jaw, holding his lean cheek in her hand.

His gaze burned. And then he pushed himself into her, easy yet ruthless at once, sheathing himself to the hilt.

For a moment—or a year, a lifetime, more—they only stared at each other, stretched out to near breaking on the edge of all that impossible sensation.

"Last time, I hurt you." His voice was gruff. Raw. Not apologetic in any way and yet it made a wet heat prick the back of Amaya's eyes. She pressed her hand that little bit harder against his face.

"Only for a moment," she whispered, as if he'd asked for her forgiveness. As if she was giving it.

And more, it was true. It had only been an instant of pain, easily forgotten and soon forgiven in the wild tumult that had followed. Even if she still didn't understand how any of that had happened. One moment they'd been talking while officially betrothed; the next their mouths had been fused together as if there was no other possibility, and the moment after that her skirts had been pulled up to her waist and he'd been buried deep inside her.

Inside her.

Amaya had understood with a vivid shock that she had no control around him—over *herself.* She'd managed *not* to have sex for twenty-three years because she'd never felt that kind of connection with anyone, and then Kavian had come along and wrecked that in a day and a half. She'd been as shocked at herself for allowing it as she had been at what had actually happened.

He was inside her again now, and this time she was far less shocked. But no more in control of either one of them. He waited, still propped there on his elbows, an enigmatic curve to that hard mouth of his.

"Go on," he murmured, as if he knew that she didn't know what to do with herself and didn't know *how* to do it anyway. Any of it. Last time had been like careening over the side of a cliff into a brilliant, cataclysmic explosion. This was no less vivid, no less overwhelming. But the explosion hovered out of reach. She thought perhaps that was his doing. His iron control. Because it certainly wasn't hers. "Find out what feels good to you, *azizty*. I want to know."

Dimly, Amaya thought that she should find this all deeply embarrassing. He seemed to read her far too well. He seemed to know too much.

He always has, a little voice whispered. *He always will*.

But Amaya ignored it, and took him at his word. She circled her hips, tentatively at first. Then, when Kavian growled in stark male approval, with more deliberation. It made a whole new fire sear its way through her as she tested out the deliriously hot sensation, the drag and the friction. She ran her hands along those delectable ridges in his torso, learning the flat, hard muscles and the carved perfection of his form, crossed here and there with scars that spoke to a life of action, lived hard. She tested the shape of his strong neck, teased his flat male nipples and licked the salt from his skin.

She pulled back, then surged forward, testing his length deep inside her, so hard in all her quivering, melting softness. Again and again and again. Until she shivered all over with a new crop of goose bumps, and looked to him, feeling something like helpless. Vibrant and electric, and still unsure.

"Allow me," Kavian said then, his voice hoarse and dark, and rich with satisfaction.

And then he dropped down closer to her, slid his hands beneath her bottom and took over.

It was the difference between the light of a candle and the blaze of the desert sun.

He took her the way he'd kissed her—all-encompassing, almost furious, dark and sweet and *necessary*. And Amaya could do nothing but wrap her arms and legs around him, hold him as tightly as she possibly could and surrender to the glory of it.

He reached between them and pressed hard at the juncture of their bodies, right where she needed it most, and she thought she heard him laugh as she shattered all around him.

But then he followed after her, right over the side of the world, and the only thing Amaya heard him call out then was her name.

CHAPTER SEVEN

It SHOULD NOT have surprised Amaya that Kavian was a man of very definite opinions, all of which he had no trouble sharing with her as he saw fit. After all, he'd never pretended otherwise.

What Amaya should wear, and when, and with whom. How she should spend her time in the palace when he was not with her, and certainly what she should do when he was. What she should eat, how often she should take walks in the extensive, terraced gardens, how much coffee she should drink and so on. There was no detail too small to escape his attention. Not because he was so controlling, he'd told her, but because they were making her his queen. A role that would be dissected by the masses of his people and a thousand tabloids the world over, so they could not gloss over the details.

"You can't really care about that," she'd said one afternoon, a bit crossly.

He'd come upon her in one of the gardens, bursting with bright pink-and-purple blossoms beneath the blue fall sky, and told her flatly that he didn't like her hair up in a ponytail. That he preferred the braid she wore over one shoulder sometimes or it loose and flowing around her as she moved.

He'd reached over and pulled the elastic from her hair

himself, then tucked it into one of his pockets, as if he couldn't bear to so much as look upon the offending ponytail a moment longer than necessary. "Can I not?"

"You have a country to run, Kavian." She'd scowled at him, and had wondered as she did where the courage to defy him so openly came from. When he still made her quake deep within. When it took everything she had. "What I'm doing with my hair should be the least of your concerns. Literally, the very least."

"I find nothing about you insignificant, *azizty*." That hint of a smile on that hard mouth of his, and it spilled through her like the desert sun above them, hot and bright, and made her think she'd do anything to see it again. Stand up to him, run, submit—whatever it took. The rush of that realization had stunned her. "None of it is beneath my notice. You are my queen."

And then he'd taken her in his arms, right there in the gardens, and kissed her until she'd decided that she had no particular allegiance to wearing her hair in a ponytail after all.

But it occurred to her—as she sat with the group of advisers who were tutoring her each day on a selection of subjects Kavian felt it was important his queen know, like proper palace protocol and the intricate social hierarchies of Daar Talaas—that she always gave in. Or he caught her and then she gave in. That it wasn't only Kavian—that her life was a series of similar surrenders that had led her straight here.

Because it had always seemed easier to bend than cause a commotion.

"You don't have the right to make that decision for me," she'd told her own father some years back. She'd wanted to take a few years off from her studies; he'd wanted her to get her degree—and he'd wanted her to stay in one place so that he'd be able to more closely monitor her, she'd suspected. She'd been very brave indeed on a mobile phone from Paris, far away from him. Polite, yet firm.

"I beg your pardon," the old sheikh had replied, and his voice had boomed down the phone line as if he'd been delivering a new edict he'd expected would become law within the hour. "I am your father and your king, Amaya. More than this, I pay your bills. Who has the right if I do not?"

And she'd acquiesced. She'd told herself that she'd simply made the practical choice. That she'd done what she had to do in the space that she'd been given. That she'd always done so as a purely rational survival tactic.

Or perhaps it's that you are a weakling, she'd snapped at herself back then, more than once, and again now as the dry and surpassingly dull vizier in front of her launched into a lecture on the importance of learning the appropriate address for visiting ambassadors. *Or you'd stand up for yourself.*

But the only person she'd openly defied in all her life was Kavian when she'd run from their betrothal—and she couldn't understand how everything had gotten so twisted since then, that she could still want to defy him with every atom in her body, fear him as much as hunger for him with every breath and yet melt at his slightest touch.

And worse, feel all that as if it was no contradiction at all.

Kavian was like all the other men in her life. Worse. They expected instant obedience not only from her, but from the whole world—and usually got it, like her late father. Her older brother, Rihad, the new king of Bakri, had been crafted from the very same mold. Even her lost brother, Omar—who'd died in a car accident while Amaya was on the run but had long been the black sheep of the

Al Bakri family because he'd refused to dutifully marry on command like the rest of them—had very much lived his life on *his* terms, no one else's.

It was only Amaya who bent. Or was it only Amaya who had to bend? It seemed the longer she spent in Kavian's intense, commanding, addictive presence, the less she knew the answer to that question.

"You are not made of rubber," Elizaveta had told her not long after her father's funeral, which Elizaveta had expected Amaya to boycott. She'd been furious that Amaya had defied her and gone to pay her respects anyway. "What happens when you cannot bend? When instead you break?"

Amaya had so desperately wanted to say, *You didn't break me, Mother. If you didn't, who could?* But she hadn't. Because it had been easier not to fight. Easier by far to simply bend.

Amaya al Bakri didn't break. She bent and she bent, and then, when she could bend no more, she ran away. There was another word to describe that kind of behavior, she often thought as she plotted escapes from Kavian's palace she knew she didn't dare attempt. *Coward.*

But she didn't feel like a coward. She felt as courageous as she felt overwhelmed every time she surrendered herself to Kavian's sensual, demanding possession, the days blending into the nights and all of it focused on his masterful touch. Was that bending? Or was she simply allowing herself to sink deep into a dizzying world of hunger and want she hadn't known existed? Where need and desire were all that mattered—despite how deeply each terrified her?

Surely the ease with which she'd given herself over to this man who'd claimed her and brought her here against her will should worry her, she thought then. She nodded along with the vizier as he gestured wildly and made points in rapid-fire Arabic that she understood more and more of by the day. Surely Kavian himself should trip every last one of her alarms.

She'd been opposed to men like him her whole life. Autocratic, overbearing, dangerous and very, very sure of themselves in all things. From what they wished to have for breakfast to what they thought Amaya should do with her life. From ponytails to polygamy.

That was why her mother had left her father, she knew—because he'd had no intention of curtailing his extramarital activity both in and out of his harem. He'd been offended when Elizaveta expressed her dismay. And that was why Amaya had spent the better part of her time on the run, furious with her brother Rihad for ordering her to marry Kavian in the first place. He had never once indicated that he understood how difficult it was for her to marry a complete stranger when he should have, having done so twice himself.

It was why she'd been certain she had to escape Kavian within moments of meeting him. Because he was *that much worse* than all the rest of them put together. That eternal, relentless imperiousness he wielded so offhandedly. That dictatorial need of his to issue commands at will and his arrogant astonishment when said commands were not immediately obeyed. That intense focus on every last, seemingly insignificant detail of *everything.* She should have been horrified by him after spending these weeks with him—as overwhelmed and trapped as she'd felt the night of their betrothal.

The trouble was that when it came to Kavian, every time he put those hard hands of his on her it was pure magic.

Maybe all men were equally magical, she reasoned. Maybe all sex was exactly the same, exactly like this. She told herself that what happened between them was probably run-of-the-mill and boring—she simply had no context by which to judge it. Because Kavian was the only man Amaya had ever known this way, ever touched this way, ever *surrendered to* in this way. Or at all.

And the truth was that she didn't find his bossiness and sheer male certainty as upsetting in the bedroom as some part of her, deep inside, insisted she should. Quite the contrary, in fact, no matter how her heart pounded at her or her head swam at the thought of him. Then again when he touched her. No matter that sheer, stunning drop into pure sensation that terrified her in retrospect and yet seemed to disappear when he hauled her against him and—

"Are you following, my lady?" The vizier's voice was an unpleasant slap back into the here and now and Amaya had to force a polite smile to cover it. "I cannot stress to you the importance of official palace protocol. It is—"

"All we have left when the world crumbles around us," Amaya finished for him, trying to sit up straighter and focus, glad she'd paid enough attention earlier to parrot that back at him. "Please, continue. I assure you I'm hanging on your every word."

The following morning Kavian rose before the sun, which Amaya had learned he did religiously. A man in his kind of peak physical condition did not happen into it by chance— he subjected himself to a rigorous fitness regime every day without fail. For hours, with what appeared to be half of his army and all their hardcore military drills.

And then, also without fail, he came back to their bed and woke her in his typically inventive, wicked style.

Sometimes with his hands. Sometimes with his mouth. Sometimes in other imaginative ways altogether.

Today he took her as she lay sprawled on her belly, one of his big hands beneath her to prop her up and hold her hips at the precise angle he wanted them, the other flat against the mattress beside her and his mouth hot on the nape of her neck.

It was blisteringly hot, wild and fast, and almost too much to bear.

"Come," he ordered her in that dark voice of his when he'd held her there on the brink for what seemed like a lifetime. When she'd lost herself completely in that desperate world of intense sensation he built so effortlessly around them, where she didn't care who was surrendering or what that might mean. "Now."

And he'd taught her so well in the weeks they'd been together. It took only that rasped command and she was gone. She wept out some kind of plea or prayer as she shattered into too many pieces to count, her face in the pillows and her hands curled into fists beside her. Then Kavian shouted out his own release and nearly threw her over once more.

He kissed her again, right there on the nape of her neck until she shuddered from the sweet kick of it all over again, and then he murmured something she didn't quite hear before he left her lying there to begin his day in earnest. It didn't matter, she thought then, dreamily suspended in that delicious in-between state where there was nothing but that sweet heat thrumming in her body. Whatever he did, however he did it, it felt like another caress.

It took her a while to rise from the bed. It took her longer to find her way into the walk-in shower that could have comfortably fit the whole of the harem he'd discarded—though that wasn't a topic she cared to think about too closely, as it led nowhere good. She stood under the hot spray and let it work its way beneath her skin.

When she was finished she wrapped herself in a silken robe so she could join him at breakfast in the sunny room directly adjoining the bedroom suite. It was the finest of his private salons, all wide-open doors to his secluded terrace and vast, sweeping views of the mountains and the desert beyond, and it struck her as she hurried into it that she was something very much like…eager.

That was a jarring thought. She told herself they'd fallen into a routine, that was all—or more accurately, he'd set one for them. He'd insisted they share these mornings from the start.

"I never know where my day will lead me," he'd said that first morning in the palace, when Amaya woke with a start to find herself draped over his chest as if she'd always shared his bed. His voice had been gruffly possessive, and he'd held her gaze to his with her hair wrapped tight around his fist, holding her head where he wanted it. "I want to know exactly where it will start, and who with."

At first she'd acquiesced because she'd been so swept away by him, by everything that had happened since she looked up to see him standing over her in that faraway café. Or that was what she'd told herself—that it was far better to lose a battle than the war. That it had nothing to do with the softness that had washed through her when he said something that might have been very nearly romantic, had he been another man. Had they been other people.

Today she recognized another truth wrapped up in that eagerness that she wanted to deny but couldn't, quite: that there was a large part of her that wanted nothing more than to sink into this life he'd laid out for her after all her years of following her mother's changeable whims and broken heart all over the planet. It was much too tempting to simply dissolve into this place, into this man, into the vision he had of her and into this life he obviously ran as smoothly and as ruthlessly as he did everything else.

It was more than tempting. It was something very much like comforting.

It feels like safety, something inside her whispered. *Like home.*

Like a note of music, played loud and long.

But she couldn't let herself think those things.

Amaya slipped into place at the glass-topped table where Kavian sat, his newspapers spread around him and his laptop open before him. Nothing about this man was safe. She knew that. Not when his gray eyes sparked silver as he gazed at her. Or when he showed her that small, dangerously compelling crook in the corner of his mouth that had become everything to her.

Though she was careful not to think of it in those terms.

"Today you will tend to your wardrobe at last," he told her, by way of greeting. "I've flown my favorite dressmakers in from Italy and they await you in the yellow parlor even now. They've brought some ready-to-wear pieces, I imagine, but will also be taking your measurements."

It took a moment for all that to sink in. Amaya jerked her attention away from his temptation of a mouth and back across the hearty breakfast Kavian preferred after his intense morning workout, set pleasingly on an array of gold and silver platters as befit a king.

"What's wrong with my wardrobe as is?" She blinked down at herself, wearing nothing but a silk wrapper and the desert breeze in her wet hair. "I don't mean this."

"I like you like this." That dark gray gaze. That responsive flip inside her chest that boded only ill. "But I would kill anyone else who saw you dressed in so little."

And she felt it again. That deep flush of pleasure, as if his *liking her* was the only thing that mattered to her—and as if he was being romantic when he said such things. It almost diverted her attention from the fact that he had *favorite dressmakers* in the first place.

"How many dresses have you had made, exactly?" she

asked him, raising her gaze to his slowly. Very slowly. "Seventeen, by any chance?"

Kavian sat there in his favorite chair with the golden morning light cascading all around him, and his slate-gray gaze seemed deeply and darkly amused the way it often did these days, though his mouth had lost that curve she craved.

"Do you truly wish me to answer that?"

"My wardrobe is perfectly adequate as it is, thank you," Amaya said quickly, as much because she really didn't want him to answer her question as because that was true. Her brother had shipped over all her things months ago, long before Kavian had caught up to her in Canada and brought her here. She'd woken up that first morning in Daar Talaas to find a separate, equally vast second closet off Kavian's sitting room stocked with everything she'd left behind in Bakri, from the gowns she'd worn to formal affairs at her brother's palace to her favorite pair of ripped black jeans from the university that she doubted Kavian would find at all appropriate. "What fault can you possibly find in it?"

"None whatsoever, were you still slinging pints in a pub in Scotland. Alas, you are not. I can assure you that while your duties will inevitably vary here, according to the needs of the people, they will never include tending a bar."

"It was a perfectly decent pub. And what do you care where I worked?"

"You were a royal princess of the House of Bakri." He had never looked like more of a king than he did then, royal and arrogant, that gaze of his a dark fire as he regarded her with some kind of astonishment. "Aside from the fact that it involved parading yourself before crowds of drunken Scotsmen every night, which your father must have been insane to allow, such a job was quite literally beneath you."

Which had been the appeal of the job, not that she was foolish enough to admit that now. Or that both Rihad and her father had read her the riot act about it, the latter almost until the day he'd died. As rebellions went, hers had been a tiny one, but it had still been hers. She couldn't regret it. She didn't.

But she'd also been relieved, somehow, when Rihad had called her to Bakri after her father died and told her it was time she took on a more formal role. She'd never had much defiance inside her. Only Kavian seemed to bring that out in her. Even now.

"You and Rihad rant on and on about my being a princess," she said then, not quite rolling her eyes at him. "It's embarrassing at best. It's nothing but a silly title from a life that was only mine for a few years when I was a child, and then again recently for my brother's political gain." Amaya shrugged. "I'm no princess. Not really. I never have been."

She couldn't read the look on his face then, and ignored the small trickle of sensation that worked its way down her spine. She didn't want to read him anyway, she assured herself as she poured out a steaming mug of coffee from the carafe at her elbow and stirred in a healthy dollop of cream. He would do as he liked either way.

It was unfortunate that she found that appealing rather than appalling.

"It is a silly title that you will no longer suffer to bear, you will be happy to learn." It was amazing that he could sound so scathing when he was still so irritatingly calm, she thought, and not for the first time. She stirred her coffee harder than necessary. "You are now a queen, Amaya. My queen, should that require clarification."

"Officially, I am only your betrothed." She shouldn't have said that, of course. That level, considering stare of his made everything inside her go still, as if she'd roused the predator in him again and was fixed in its sights. "I've been learning a great deal about the traditional Daar Talaas palace hierarchy in the classes you've made me take."

"They are not classes." His voice was as dangerously soft as his gaze was severe. "You are not a fractious adolescent who has been dispatched to some kind of summer school in place of the detention she clearly deserves."

She really did roll her eyes then. "Lectures, then. Is that a better term?"

"You are meeting with your aides and advisers to better understand and shape your role as queen of this great land." The way he arched those dark brows at her dared her to contradict him. "Just as you are practicing your Arabic so you may converse with the subjects under your rule whenever appropriate."

He meant *when fully vetted by my men*. When it came to any issue that could be construed as pertaining to her physical safety, Amaya had found that Kavian was utterly inflexible. Unlike the rest of the time, when he was only *almost* utterly inflexible. Which should not have amused her, surely. Where was her panic?

What happens when you cannot bend? her mother had demanded, and what did it matter what Elizaveta's motivations for asking had been? *When instead you break?*

"The point is that the role of 'princess,' whatever that means, was never one I learned to play," she said instead, because she couldn't sort out was happening inside her. Because she was afraid this was what *broken* looked like, this absurd idea that she could be safe with a man this elemental, this raw and powerful. "I was never treated as a princess of anything anywhere we went after my mother and I left Bakri."

Quite the opposite, she thought then as the memories she usually kept locked away rushed back at her, thick and fast. There had been a long stretch of years when Elizaveta would fly into one of her cold furies at the very sound of the word *princess* and punish Amaya for it whether or not she'd been the one to say it out loud.

She took a sip of the thick coffee and tried to swallow the unpleasant past down with the dark Arabian brew. "If anything, my mother downplayed it as much as possible."

That shrug of his was still a cool, harsh weapon, and then he turned his attention back to the papers before him, which only made it worse. "Because you outrank her."

The shrug was a weapon and the words a blow.

For a moment, Amaya simply reeled. She placed her mug back down on the glass table very, very carefully. She blinked.

"My mother doesn't care about rank," she said, and she couldn't have said why her voice sounded like that, as if there were rough and terrible things simmering there beneath the surface. "She walked away from Bakri of her own volition. If she cared about rank she would have stayed in the place where she was queen, not taken off into the big, bad world where she had no means of support."

"No means of support?" Kavian shook his head when she frowned at him in confusion. "She had a walking, talking bank account at her disposal. She had you."

That sensation of reeling, of actual spinning, only worsened. "What are you talking about?"

"You," he said very distinctly, his gaze a fierce shot of intense gray in the bright room, "are the daughter of a king. Your mother did not live by her wits or her charm or even her looks, Amaya. She lived off the trust your father set up in your name, for your support."

Amaya couldn't speak. Or move. She felt as if he'd hammered a giant nail straight into her and pinned her to her chair.

She thought of all the times Elizaveta had lectured her about her *expectations*, her terrible *entitlement*. She remembered the many, many times her mother had embarrassed her in front of others by claiming that Amaya was "her father's daughter," in a manner meant to suggest Amaya always selfishly wanted far more than her share, that she was greedy and ill-bred, that she was entirely, deliberately heedless of reality. She'd excused these things, one after the next, because she'd understood where her mother was coming from, what Amaya's father had done. She'd assumed these things came from her mother's panic at having to find ways to support them all on her own.

"I treat you like an adult because you would otherwise grow up coddled and spoiled like every other member of the Bakri line," Elizaveta had said when Amaya was perhaps eleven. "The truth is that we have nothing. We are dependent on the kindness of friends."

She'd meant her many lovers, the men who she'd never stayed with for too long, because they had always required such careful handling to put up with a woman with a sulky daughter in tow. Or so Elizaveta had always claimed.

"I don't expect you to be as grateful as you should— that's your father's influence in you, I'm sure—but you must comprehend what there is to lose if you don't do as I say." Elizaveta had glared at Amaya as if she'd expected her daughter to argue, when Amaya had long since learned the folly of that kind of thing. Even then, even as a child, she'd known it was better to bend to those who could not. "We'll lose everything. The roof above your head and the clothes on your back. Is that what you want?"

That had not been what eleven-year-old Amaya had wanted. The very idea had given her nightmares. And Elizaveta had never been a perfect parent, certainly. Life with her had always been complicated, but Amaya had been sympathetic because she'd understood that her mother hadn't said those things to be cruel. Amaya's father had broken something inside her, and sometimes it came out as poison. Amaya had learned not to take it personally... Or anyway, she'd tried her best not to take it personally.

"You are mistaken," Amaya said to Kavian now when she could speak without that rough-edged thing inside her taking over and revealing too much. "I don't know where you heard such a thing."

"Had she married any of the men she found, she would have had to return you to your father and worse, to her way of thinking, give up her access to your money." Another shrug, which made her want to throw her plate at him. A flicker in that gray gaze made her think he knew it, too. "This is not an attack, Amaya. This is simply a fact. I did not hear this through some grapevine or other—I've seen the paperwork."

Amaya shook her head, so hard it almost hurt, and noticed her heart had started to kick at her, almost as if she was panicked.

"My mother was a self-made woman. She had nothing when she left Ukraine. She talked her way from minor dance halls into the fashion houses of Milan. She had nothing *but* her wit, her charm and her looks. That was how she entered her marriage to my father, and that was how she left it. If anything, I was a complication."

It was only when she was finished speaking that Amaya realized her voice had risen, as if every sentence were a plate thrown, a blow landed on his wholly impervious form.

"She also had ambition," Kavian said softly. He was so much more dangerous the quieter he got, she knew. She sucked in a breath against it. "Never forget that. She left Bakri because she was losing the sheikh's favor. Better to leave and tell a sad tale across the years to a thousand receptive audiences. Better by far to hold the king's daughter as ransom than to remain in Bakri as a neglected, forgotten wife. The sheikh would have banished her to one of the outlying residences, far away from the palace where she would wither away into irrelevance, and she knew it. That, *azizty*, did not suit your mother's ambitions at all."

Amaya stared at him, willing herself not to react in the way she suspected he wanted her to do. Her lips felt bloodless. Her stomach twisted—hard. "You don't know anything about my mother. She was not ambitious. She was in love."

She shouldn't have said that. She shouldn't have uttered those words. Not to him, not here. Not out loud—and she didn't dare ask herself why that was. But Amaya couldn't take them back, no matter how much she wished she could. She couldn't make that taut, near-painful silence between them disappear, or do anything about that sudden arrested look on Kavian's austere face. She straightened in her seat instead, and forced herself to meet that edgy gray gaze of his straight on as if she felt nothing at all.

"My father was a convincing man when it suited him." She heard that catch in her throat and she knew Kavian did, too, but she pushed on. "He convinced a woman who had been born with nothing and raised to expect little else that he adored her. That he worshipped her. That he would remake his world in her honor."

She didn't point out how familiar that sounded. Just as she didn't give that searing blast of temper in Kavian's dark gaze a chance to form into harsh words on his lips.

"He lied. Maybe he meant it when he said it—what do I know? But my mother believed him. That was why she thought there was something she could do to regain his favor, to win back his attention once it drifted. Anything to make him love her again. But what my father truly loved was collecting, Kavian. He was always looking for his next acquisition. He didn't lose much sleep over the things he'd already collected and shunted aside."

He didn't speak for a long, cool moment that careened around inside Amaya's chest, leaving jagged marks. She tilted up her chin and told herself she could handle it. *Him.* Or survive it, anyway.

"Is that what you're afraid of?" he asked.

She would never know how she held his gaze. How she managed to keep herself from reacting to that terrible, infinitely destructive question. She only knew that she did it. That she stared back at him, stone to his stone, as if her life depended on it.

"Are you talking about your mother, Amaya?" Kavian pushed at her in that quiet way of his that nonetheless made every bone in her body ache. She fought to restrain a shiver. "Or yourself?"

"Don't tie yourself in knots looking for comparisons that don't exist," she managed to bite out at him, still channeling stone and steel and *calm*. "I'm nothing like her."

"I am aware. If you were, you would not be here." She hated the way he looked at her as if knew all the things she carried inside, her memories and her dreams and her darkest secrets alike. As if what Kavian enjoyed collecting was every last piece of her soul. And once he had them all, she couldn't help wondering then in a panic, what would become of it? Or her? "And as fascinating as this conversation is, it doesn't alter the fact that you require an entirely new wardrobe. You must look like my queen whether you feel like it or do not. Especially at our wedding ceremony, which, I hesitate to remind you, is in a matter of weeks."

"I don't want a ceremony."

"I didn't ask you what you wanted. I told you what

was necessary and what I require." His gaze glinted with amusement then, and that was much worse. It moved in her like heat. Like need. "Shall I demonstrate to you why you should begin to learn the distinction between the two? And the consequences if you do not?"

But Kavian's consequences always ended the same way—with Amaya stretched out naked on the edge of some or other gloriously intense pleasure she worried she might not survive, begging him for mercy and forgetting her own damn name. So she only picked up her coffee again and took another sip, schooling her features into something serene enough to be vaguely regal and ignoring that wicked crook of his hard mouth as she did it.

"A new wardrobe fit for a queen?" she murmured, her voice cool and smooth. Stone and steel. Just like him. "How delightful. I can't wait."

"I am so pleased you think so," Kavian said in the very same tone, though his gray eyes gleamed. "We leave for your first public appearance as queen tomorrow morning. I'm thrilled you'll be able to dress the part at last."

"As am I," she said dryly. Almost as if she couldn't help herself—couldn't keep herself from needling him. "I have worried about little else."

"Ah, *azizty*," he murmured, sounding as close to truly amused as she'd ever heard him, "when will you understand? I am not a man who does anything by halves."

CHAPTER EIGHT

IF HE WAS a good man, Kavian reflected the following day, he would not have set up his betrothed for this particular day of tests. He would not have tested her at all. Had it been about what he wanted, he simply would have kept her in his bed forever. He would have lost himself there in the sweet madness of her scent, the addiction of her smooth skin. The glory he'd found in her arms that shook him far more than he cared to admit.

But this was Daar Talaas and Kavian had never been good. He'd never had the chance to try. He was the king, and thus he did what was necessary for his people. If that happened to align with what was good, so be it. But he would not lose sleep over it if it did not.

He would sleep like an innocent, he assured himself, whatever happened in the desert that had forged him. It would be the making of Amaya, too, he knew. There was no other way.

After all, she had already taken the news of her mother's true treatment of her in stride. Kavian dared to allow himself a shred of optimism that she would rise to whatever occasion presented itself.

They'd left the palace in the morning, taking a helicopter out to the stable complex on the far side of the treacherous northern mountains. They'd stood together in the center of the courtyard while his men, a sea of servants and stable hands, and a selection of his finest Arabian horses hurried all around them.

"Do you ride?" he'd asked, almost as an afterthought.

She'd been dressed like a Daar Talaasian noblewoman, in an exquisite dress that adhered to desert custom with her arms and legs covered and her head demurely veiled. It only made her every graceful movement that much more intoxicating, to Kavian's mind, because he had the pleasure of knowing what was beneath. All her soft skin, the temptation of her hair, the sweet taste of her, woman and cream. But there'd been no veiling that cool gaze of hers, dark chocolate mixed with ice as it met his.

"I've ridden a horse before, if that's what you mean. I'm sure you already know that my mother and I spent several summers on a ranch in Argentina."

What he knew was far less interesting to him than what she chose to tell him. "Did you fall off a great deal?"

She stiffened almost imperceptibly, and those marvelous bittersweet eyes of hers narrowed. "Are you asking me if I've suffered a head injury?"

He'd kept himself from smiling by sheer force of will, and it was much harder than it should have been. Much harder than he could recall it ever having been before. "I am asking if I can expect you to topple off the side of a horse while you are meant to be riding it."

"Not on purpose," she'd retorted, and it had only occurred to him then that they weren't in private any longer. That his men stood around him, closely watching this exchange with the scandalous woman who had evaded him for months—whom he had clearly not yet subdued. "Do you plan to ride me out into the desert, throw me to the sand dunes and then *claim* I fell off?"

They had been speaking in English, which was lucky

as very few of his men understood a word of it. The fact that he'd been nearly smiling at her in obvious indulgence, however, was less lucky. Any softness, any hint of a crack in his armor, would be exploited as a weakness by his enemies. Kavian knew that all too well.

He couldn't have said why he cared so much less in that moment than he should have.

He'd given the order then. It had taken only a few moments for the small party to mount up, and when he'd looked back down at Amaya she'd been standing there, doing an admirable job of keeping herself from frowning at him. He'd seen the effort she expended in the way her dark eyes crinkled in the corners.

"Did you ask me all those questions for your own amusement?"

"Yes," he'd replied dryly. "I am a hilarious king. Ask anyone."

And then he'd simply reached down from the back of his horse, clamped an arm around her middle and hauled her up before him.

He'd felt more than heard the tiny noise she made, somewhere between a gulp and a squeak, and he knew that had he found her pulse with his mouth, it would be going wild. Yet she only gripped the arm he'd banded around her abdomen and said nothing.

"Courage, *azizty,*" he'd murmured, his voice low and for her ears only. "Today you must prove you are the queen my people deserve."

"But—"

"Whether you wish it or do not. This is about Daar Talaas, Amaya, not you or me."

He'd felt the breath she'd sucked in and he'd thought she'd planned to argue further, but she hadn't. She'd been quiet. Perhaps too quiet, but there'd been nothing he could do about it then—or would have done if he could, if he was honest with himself. A test could hardly matter if it was without some peril. So instead, he'd given the next order and they'd ridden out into the desert, deep into the far reaches of the desolate northern territories.

It was not an easy ride by any means, but Amaya did not complain, which pleased Kavian greatly. She did not squirm against him, nor divert his attention any more than the simple fact of her there between his legs, her pert bottom snug against the hardest part of him as they rode, distracted him.

He found it impossible not to notice that she fit him perfectly.

They reached the encampment by midafternoon, after hours spent galloping across the shifting sands, racing against the sun itself at this time of year. Fierce men on bold horses met them some distance away and led them the rest of the way in, shouting ahead in their colorful local dialect. The collection of tents that waited for them had the look of a makeshift traveling camp instead of a permanent settlement, despite the goats and children who roamed in and around the grounds and told a different tale. Kavian knew that it was all a deliberate, canny bit of sleight of hand. The truth was in the quality of the horseflesh, the presence of so many complacent and well-fed camels, the fine, sturdy fabric of the tents themselves.

It could have been a scene from any small village out here in the desert, unchanged in centuries, and there was a part of Kavian that would always long for the simplicity of this life. No palace, no intrigue. No political necessities, no alliances and no greater enemy than the harsh environment. Just the thick heat of the desert sun above, the vastness and the quiet all around and a tent to call his home.

Though he knew that was not the truth of this place, either.

"What are we doing here?" Amaya asked as they rode into camp, and he wondered what she saw. The dirt, the dust. The sand in everything. The rich, dark scent in the air that announced the presence of the tribe's livestock, horses and camels. The suspicious frowns from the people who could see at a glance that she was not one of them. The lack of anything even resembling an amenity.

There was no oasis to cool off in here, because it was another fifteen minutes or so farther north, fiercely guarded and zealously protected for the use of this tribe alone—but Amaya couldn't know that. The women who clustered around the fire, beginning their preparations for the evening meal, eyed them as their party approached but made no move to welcome them, and Kavian imagined how they must look to Amaya. But he knew what she could not—that their seeming poverty was as feigned as the rest.

Nothing was ever quite what it seemed. He came here as often as he could to remember that.

"I have come a very long way to have a conversation," Kavian told his betrothed, and that, too, was only a part of it.

"To settle a dispute?" Amaya asked. She didn't wait for him to confirm or deny. "The king himself would hardly ride out to discuss the weather, I suppose."

Kavian pulled on the horse's reins, bringing the Thoroughbred to a dancing stop in front of a line of stern-faced elders, all of whom bowed deep at the sight of him. He inclined his head, then swung down from the horse's back, leaving his hand resting possessively on Amaya's leg as he stood beside her.

He greeted the men before him, introduced Amaya as

his betrothed queen and then they all performed the usual set of formal greetings and offers of hospitality. It went back and forth for some time, as expected. Only when the finest tent belonging to the village's leader had been offered and accepted, as was custom, did Kavian turn to Amaya again and lift her down from the horse.

"That wasn't the Arabic I know," she said, in soft English that sounded far sweeter than the look in her eyes. "I caught only one or two words in ten."

He didn't laugh, though he felt it move in him. "Let me guess which ones."

"Did you accept the man's kind offer of a girl for your use?" she asked, and though her voice was cool, her eyes glittered. "They must have heard you'd gone from seventeen concubines to one. A tremendous national tragedy indeed."

He could have put her mind at ease. He could have told her that the girl, like so many of the girls he was offered in these far-off places that never advanced much with the times, was little more than a child. He had taken many of them back to the palace, installed them in his harem and given them a much better life—one that had never included his having sex with them. He could have told Amaya that such girls accounted for most—though not all, it was true; he had never been a saint by any measure—of the harem he'd kept. He could have told her that there had never been any possibility that he would take a young girl as his due tonight and more, that the elders had known that, hence the extravagant effusiveness of their offers.

But he did not.

"They approve my choice of bride and have offered us a place to stay," he replied instead, his voice even. "More or less. It will not be a palace, but it will have to do."

She blinked as if he'd insulted her. Perhaps he had.

"I'm not the one accustomed to palaces," she reminded him, her voice still calm, though he could feel the edge in it as if it were a knife she dragged over his skin. "I keep telling you, I was only ever a princess in name. Perhaps you should be worried about how you'll manage a night somewhere that isn't drenched in gold and busy with servants to cater to your every need. *I* have slept under bushes while hiking across Europe, when it was necessary. I've camped almost everywhere. *I* will be fine."

He wanted to crush her in his arms. He wanted to take that mouth of hers with his, and who cared what was appropriate or who was watching or what he had to prove? He wanted to lose himself inside her forever. But he could do none of those things. Not here.

Not yet.

"I will also be fine, *azizty*," he said, his voice blunt with all these things he wanted that he couldn't have. Not now. "I grew up here."

Kavian strode off and left Amaya standing there, all by herself in what was truly the middle of nowhere, as if he hadn't dropped that bomb on her at all. He didn't look back as he disappeared into a three-sided tent structure with a group of stern-faced men. He didn't so much as pause.

And for a wild moment, Amaya's pulse leaped and she thought about running again now that she was finally out of his sight—but then she remembered where she was. There had been *nothing*, all afternoon. Nothing but the great desert in every direction, which she'd found she hadn't hated as she'd expected she would. But that didn't mean she wanted to lose herself in it.

She had no idea how Kavian had located this place without a map today, just as she had no idea what he'd meant. How could he have grown up *here*? So far away from the world and his own palace? Her brothers had been raised in royal splendor, waited on by battalions of servants, educated by fleets of the best tutors from all over the world before being sent off to the finest schools. Amaya supposed she'd thought that all kings were created in the same way.

It occurred to her, standing there all alone in the middle of the vast desert that Kavian was clearly bound to in ways she didn't understand, that she didn't know much about this man who had claimed her—even as he seemed to know her far too well. And better every day whether she liked it or not.

You do like it, a small voice whispered. *You like that he notices* everything. *You like that he sees* you. But she dismissed it.

Kavian had marched off with those men as if he was a rather more hands-on sort of king than her brother or father had ever been. Amaya assumed, when she shifted to see the women watching her from their place by the central fire, that she was meant to be the same sort of queen. No lounging about beneath palm trees eating cakes and honey, or adhering to the stiffly formal royal protocols in place at her brother's palace. No disappearing into the tent that had been set aside for them and collapsing on the nearest fainting couch. All of those options were appealing, and were certainly what her own mother would have done in her place, but she understood that none of them would win her any admirers here.

You run, she reminded herself. *That's who you are. Why not do that here? Or do the next best thing—hide?*

But she hated the notion that that was precisely what Kavian expected her to do. That he believed she really was some kind of fluttery princess who couldn't handle herself. It was so infuriating that Amaya ignored the waiting tent, ignored what her own body was telling her to do. Instead, she made her way over to the group of women and set about making herself useful.

When Kavian finally returned to the center of camp with that same cluster of men hours later, Amaya found she was proud of the fact that the evening meal was ready and waiting for him, as the encampment's honored guest. It wasn't the sort of feast he'd find served in his well-appointed salons, but she'd helped make it with her own hands. There was grilled lamb, a special treat because the king had come, and hot, fresh flatbread the women had made in round pans they'd settled directly in the coals. There was a kind of fragrant rice with vegetables mixed in. There were dates and homemade cheeses wrapped in soft cloths. It was far more humble than anything in the palace, perhaps, and there was no gold or silver to adorn it, but Amaya rather thought that added to the simple meal's appeal.

The men settled down around the serving platters and ate while the women waited and watched from a distance, as was the apparent custom. It was not until the two old men who sat with Kavian drank their coffee together that the village seemed to relax, because, one of the women Amaya had come to know over the long afternoon told her in the half Arabic, half hand gestures language they'd cobbled together as they'd gone along, that meant the king had settled the dispute.

Amaya ate when the women did, all of them sitting on a common mat near one of the tents, in a kind of easy camaraderie she couldn't remember ever feeling before. Out here in the desert, they didn't have to understand every word spoken to understand each other. It didn't take a common language to puzzle out group dynamics.

Amaya knew that the older woman with the wise eyes whom the others treated with a certain deference watched

her more closely than the others did. She knew exactly
when she'd gotten *that* woman to smile in the course of
their shared labors, and she hadn't been entirely sure why
she'd felt that like such a grand personal triumph. Or why
she'd laughed more with these women she'd only met
this afternoon and only half understood than she had in
years.

The night wore on, pressing down from all sides—the
stars so bright they seemed to be right there within reach,
dancing on the other side of the fire. It reminded her of that
winter in New Zealand, but even there the nearby houses
had cast some light to relieve the sprawl of the Milky Way
and its astonishing weight up above. Not so here. There
was no light but the fire and the pipes the men smoked
as they talked. There was nothing but the immensity of
the heavens above, the great twisting fire of the galaxy.
It pressed its way deep into Amaya's heart, until it ached
as if it were broken wide-open or smashed into pieces.
Both, perhaps.

"You did well," Kavian said when he came to fetch her
at last. He reached down and pulled her to her feet, making the other women cluck and sigh, in a manner that required no translation.

"They think you're very romantic," she said, and she
didn't know why she felt something like bashful, as if she
thought so, too. Or worse—wistful.

"They think we are newly wed," he corrected her. "And
still foolish with it."

"It's the same thing, really." She tilted her head up to
look him in the eye as best she could in all the tumultuous
dark. "Either way, it's not expected to last."

She thought he meant to say something then, but he
didn't, and she didn't know why it felt like a rebuke. She
had to repress a shiver at the sudden drop in heat as he led

her away from the group, the flames, the laughter. She felt a sharp pang as she went, as if she was losing something. As if she would never get it back—as if it was so much smoke on a Bedouin fire, curling its way into the messy night sky above them. Lost in the night, never to return.

Amaya made herself breathe. Told herself it was the thick night, that was all, making everything seem that much more raw and poignant than it was.

There were lanterns guiding their way through the cluster of tents, and Kavian's strong body against the impenetrable darkness that pressed in like ink on all sides, but that didn't change the way she felt. It didn't help that ache inside.

If anything, it intensified it.

"I am told you impressed the women," Kavian said as he pulled back the flap and ushered her into the unpretentious tent that was theirs for the night. She felt as nervous as she had in the baths that first day in Daar Talaas, Amaya realized. She walked ahead of him, running her gaze over the bed flat on the floor but plumped up high and piled with linens, the serviceable rug that looked handwoven, the fine pillows scattered on the floor to mark a cozy seating area and a collection of lanterns that made it all seem deeply romantic. And she was astonished at how much she wanted it to be. "That is no easy task."

"Did you imagine I would cower in the tent?"

"I accepted that was a possibility. You did once secrete yourself amongst my shoes."

"One of the gifts of having moved somewhere new every time my mother felt like it, is that I'm good with groups of strangers," Amaya said. She made herself turn and face him, and she was surprised at how hard that was with so much tumult inside her. "It's that or no one speaks to you for months on end."

"There is being friendly and then there is helping cook a meal for the whole camp." Kavian still stood near the entrance, his gray eyes searching hers. "They are not the same thing."

"You told me I was to act as your queen."

"And you take direction, do you? How novel." He eyed her, but she couldn't let herself respond. Not when she had no idea what it was that held her in its grip. "Does a queen normally tend a cooking fire and sit in the dirt with strangers?"

"This one did," she retorted, not sure why she was trembling. Why she couldn't stop. His hard mouth crooked slightly. Very slightly. It didn't help at all.

"I am a man of war, Amaya," Kavian said softly. "I need a queen who can get her hands dirty. Who is not troubled by palace protocol when the palace is nowhere in sight. You please me, my queen. You please me deeply."

Something turned over, deep inside her. "I'm not your queen."

"Now you contradict yourself."

"I think you're confused because I cooked for you. Like a real person."

That gleam in his eyes turned them a polished silver in the soft light. And she couldn't tell him that what had really happened was first that she'd wanted to defy his low expectations—and then that she'd wanted to make him proud.

Here, today, she'd *wanted* to be his queen. She couldn't *say* that. She couldn't admit it to him when she could hardly accept it herself.

"Are we not real?" he asked. Almost gently.

Her throat felt too tight. "Things aren't the same in the palace, are they? It's a *palace*."

"A palace is a building made of carefully chosen stone and the concentrated artisanship of hundreds of loyal subjects across decades," Kavian said quietly. Intently. "It is a monument to the hopes of my people, their desire for unity and strength against all that might come at them. As am I. As are you, too. It could not be any more real than that."

"But you said you grew up here, not there."

He moved farther into the tent and she watched as he unwrapped his traditional headdress, then shrugged out of his robes, stripping down until he wore nothing but a pair of boxer briefs low on his narrow hips. He should have looked like a normal, regular, everyday man, she thought with something like despair. He was in his underwear in a tent in the middle of nowhere. Surely that should...*reduce* him, somehow.

But this was Kavian. And today, she'd wanted to please him. To be the queen he wanted. Looking at him here, she understood that suicidal urge.

He better resembled a god than any mere man. It was as if he'd been hewn from the finest marble and then breathed into life. His skin gleamed like old gold in the lantern light and she couldn't read a thing on his face as he came toward her. Nor when he reached for her.

He unwound her scarves from her as if he was unwrapping a precious gift. Slowly. Reverently. He combed his fingers through her hair when it tumbled down, then helped her out of the long, traditional dress she'd been given yesterday by his dressmakers. When she wore nothing but her slip, a basic thing that wasn't meant to be at all alluring, his gaze heated, but still he did nothing but gently rake his fingers through her hair.

It was almost as if it calmed him as much as it did her.

"My uncle was the king of Daar Talaas when I was born," he told her, so softly she thought at first he hadn't meant to speak at all. "He was a good ruler and the people loved him, but despite the wives he took and the many concubines he kept, he had no sons. So when he died, the throne passed to his younger brother. My father."

He wasn't looking at her. His attention was on the thick fall of her dark hair that he wrapped around and around his hand instead, then let unravel again. Yet Amaya found she could hardly breathe.

"My father was a young man with two wives, one renowned for her fertility, the other for her beauty." His gaze was dark when it met hers. Something like tortured, she'd have said. "His first wife had given him four sons already, my half brothers. The people were pleased, for my father and his wealth of sons ensured that the throne would remain in the hands of our family, come what may. That meant stability."

"What about you?" she asked. "Were you considered part of that wealth?"

He did not smile. If anything, his gaze darkened.

"My mother was a fragile woman who had nothing but her beauty and, perhaps because of it, a great envy for all the things she felt she was owed," he said, in the cool tones of someone who was telling a distant myth, a legend. Not his own family's story. *His* story. That shook through Amaya, but she didn't move. She didn't speak. "She was far more pleasing to my father in bed than his first wife had ever been, but even when she had me, she could not compete with the simple fact of her rival's four healthy heirs. My father's first wife was a simple woman, without my mother's looks or cleverness, but none of this mattered. She was the queen. She was revered. My mother came second, and I, her only child, fifth."

Amaya might have realized only today that there were a great many things she didn't know about this man, but she did know that he didn't have any family. Everyone knew that. Which made her heart stutter in her chest, because this story could be headed only one horrible way.

She reached over and pressed her hand against the hard plane of the muscle that covered his heart, and her breath began to shake when he slid his hand over hers and held it there.

"You don't have to tell me this story," she said, and her voice was barely a whisper. "I didn't mean to dredge up bad memories."

"My mother took a lover," Kavian said by way of reply. His voice was so dark, leading them inexorably toward a terrible end. She could see that much on his face. She could feel it in the air around them, crushing her in a tense fist, but she made herself stand tall. If he could tell it, she could take it. She promised herself she could. "He was one of my father's ministers, ambitious and amoral. But he was not content to simply defile my father's wife. He wanted the throne."

"How could he take it? Was he related to you?"

"The throne of Daar Talaas is held by the man who can hold it." Kavian did not so much say that as *intone* it. "So it is written in the stones on which the throne itself sits. So it has always been."

Amaya had to press her palm that much harder against him, to remind herself he was real. Flesh and blood, not a statue in a palace hewn from rock. Not etched stones beneath an old throne. Far more than the story he was telling her. Far more than the darkness that was pouring from him now, his eyes and his voice alike.

"I don't know what that means." It was more that she didn't *want* to know. But she didn't look away.

"It means that while families often hold on to the throne for some generations, this is because they tend to consolidate their power, not because there is a blood requirement."

He shifted, which made his previous stillness seem that much more extreme by comparison. "My mother's lover was no fool. He knew he could not take the throne by force. The Daar Talaas army cannot be manipulated. They serve the throne, not the man."

He had never looked as distant as he did then. Bleak and uncompromising. He stepped back, Amaya's hand fell to her side, and she thought she'd never felt so empty.

Yet Kavian kept going. "He slit my father's throat as he sat at the dinner table, in a place where there is meant to be only peace, even between enemies. Then he killed my brothers, one by one. Then both of my father's wives, including my mother. Especially my mother, I should say. Because even the man she colluded with hated that she was traitorous enough to betray her own husband. Her own king."

"Why did he spare you?" She hardly recognized her voice.

That wasn't a smile he aimed at her then. It was far too painful. It cut too deep.

"My mother had a servant girl who she did not so much trust as fail to notice. The girl knew of my mother's lover and enough of the plans they made that when the first alarm sounded, she ran. She took me out of the palace and claimed I was her own."

Amaya knew who he meant immediately. "The woman with the wise eyes. All the other women looked to her today."

"She is the wife of the chief here," Kavian said, but there was a flicker in his gaze that told her she'd impressed him, and it warmed her. It more than warmed her. "Back then, however, she took a terrible risk in bringing me to her father's tent, alone and unwed, with a toddler she could not prove was the king's missing son. The elders might not have believed her. She risked her life and her family's honor to save me."

"But they believed her."

"They did." He studied her face. "And they are simple people here, not aristocrats with agendas. Good people who follow the old ways. Blood begets blood, Amaya. They raised me to avenge my family, as was my right and responsibility as its only remaining member."

Amaya couldn't speak for a long moment. She thought of a tiny boy who'd lost everything and had been given only vengeance in return, out here in this harsh, desolate place without a single hint of softness. It made her heart hurt, as if he were the great sky pressing into her, as impossible and as far away. As beautiful and as untouchable.

He had been a lost child and they had made him into a stone. And now he thought it was a virtue.

"I'm sorry," she said softly. "That seems like an undue burden to place on a child."

"You misunderstand me." His gaze was too dark. His eyes glittered. "I am not telling you this story because I regret what happened to me. What is there to regret? I was lucky."

"You are also now the king."

"I am."

"Does that mean…" She searched his face, but he might truly have been made of marble then. He was that unyielding. "Blood begat blood?"

"It means that I grew up," Kavian said quietly. With a deep ferocity that tugged at her in ways she didn't understand, as if his story was changing things inside her as he told it. Shifting them. "It means that I dedicated myself to becoming the necessary weapon to achieve my ends. And it means that when I had the chance, I exacted my vengeance, and know this, Amaya, if you know nothing else about me. My single regret is that the man who murdered my family could die but once."

CHAPTER NINE

IT WAS A TEST, Kavian reminded himself harshly. The most important one.

This had all been a test. The long ride into the most remote part of the Daar Talaas Desert, abandoning her to see what she would do under the watchful eye of the woman he'd long considered his real mother. Then this. Throwing out the bloody truth of his family and his own dark deeds to see what she would make of them.

To see what Amaya was made of, after all. Who she really was when there was nowhere to run. If she was, truly, the one woman who could embody all he wanted.

Kavian stood there, stone-faced before this woman he had chased across the world, and awaited her reaction. It would determine the whole of their future.

He told himself he didn't care either way. That his heart was as much stone as he knew his expression was. There were some who had found his pursuit of vengeance unforgivable. There were others whose interest in his past had always seemed *too* avid for his comfort. This was nothing but a test to see where Amaya would fall on that spectrum.

It would set the stage for how he handled his marriage going forward, nothing more. Either she would prove herself a worthy queen, a woman like his foster mother, who was braver than most men, *his queen*—or she would sim-

ply be a wife with a lofty title who would eventually give
Kavian his heirs.

It matters little which way she goes, he told himself
then.

But he found that he was frozen in place, awaiting her
judgment, all the same.

Amaya swallowed hard, but she didn't shift her gaze
from his. She still stood tall before him. The warm light
from the lanterns made her look gilded, standing there with
her glorious spill of dark hair all around her and her perfect breasts visible beneath that silky little shift she wore.
She was still so pretty it almost felt like an attack. An as-
sault. It rolled over him and flattened him. It took out his
defenses like a kick to the knees.

But he had no intention of showing her that.

"You obviously expect me to clutch at my pearls and
faint," she said after a long, long moment.

"Aim for the bed," he advised her. "The rug is not as
soft as it appears."

"Did you torture him?" she asked.

He hadn't expected that. He considered her more closely.

"No," he said at last. "He was the butcher. I wanted only
what he took. If not my family, then the throne."

"Did it change you?"

He blinked, and ignored that heavy thing inside his
chest that seemed to bear down hard at that, as if his heart
was still wrapped in those same old chains.

As if he was.

"No," he said after a moment, when that harsh pull
inside him faded. Or became more bearable somehow.
"The change you mean happened much earlier. When I
accepted that I would become what I hated in order to
do what I must. I do not regret avenging my family. I regret only that I share anything with the man who killed

them—that in order to honor my family I became a murderer, just like him."

"No." Her voice was fierce then, immediate, and her eyes glittered. "Nothing like him. You could never be anything like him. He killed children for his own selfish gain. All you did was take out a monster."

And Kavian had not realized, not until that moment, how very much he'd needed to hear her say that. How much he'd needed proof that she was who he'd thought she was from the start. He didn't want to analyze it. He didn't want to consider the implications. To hell with all that.

She was looking at him as if he was some kind of hero. Not the monster he'd long ago accepted he'd had to become because he'd had no other choice. She was looking at him as if—

But he couldn't let himself go too far down that road. He couldn't risk it.

"Come here," he gritted out at her, and he didn't smile when she jerked slightly at the harsh command, or even when she obeyed. He crossed his arms over his chest and peered down at her as she drew near. "Kiss me."

Amaya swayed toward him, the light playing off the silken shine of her shift and the smooth intoxication of her skin. She hooked one hand over his forearm where it crossed the other, and then she went up on her toes and slid her other hand along his jaw as if she sought to comfort him. And he felt the wholly uncharacteristic urge to lean into her palm, as if she was sunlight and he could bask in her a while.

Just a little while, something in him urged.

"Does this mean I passed your test, Kavian?" she asked him, a smile in those dark chocolate eyes and teasing the corners of her lips. "Or are there more hoops I must leap through tonight?"

He smiled then. Triumph and need and that heavy thing in his chest that made his heart beat too fast, too hard. He didn't want to name it. He refused.

"It means I want you to kiss me," he said, as if hunger for her weren't tearing at him, deeper and more ravenous than any he'd ever felt before. As if he could stand here all night, ignoring it. "I do not believe I was unclear."

"A kiss is my only reward for hours on a horse and hard labor by the fire?" She was teasing him again. Kavian understood that, even though he rather thought she took her life in her hands when she dared do it. Or maybe that was his life she held, and she was squeezing it much too hard as she went. So hard, it was almost a struggle to breathe. "That hardly seems equal to the effort I put out today to please you. Shouldn't you be the one to please me for a change?"

"Kiss me," he suggested, darkly, "and you will find out exactly how pleasing I can be, *azizty*."

She didn't laugh, though he felt it there in the air between them, music and magic, as if she had. She hooked her other hand around his neck and stretched herself up toward him, and he let her. He waited.

Amaya hovered there for a moment, her mouth a scant breath from his, her dark gaze solemn. Kavian remembered, suddenly, their first meeting. That same look in her eyes as they'd met his for the first time. The promises she'd made him then.

And that next morning, when her brother had come to tell him that she had fled the palace, her whereabouts unknown.

"If you break another vow, Amaya, I will not be quite so forgiving." He hadn't meant to speak. He hardly knew his own voice when he did.

But her lips curved slightly, only slightly, and she didn't pull away. "Has this been your version of forgiving?"

He could hardly hear her over the thunder of his own heart.

"You'll understand if I find that confusing."

"You are the only living creature I have ever forgiven anything."

It was a confession, gruff and unexpected. And he should not have made it to her, Kavian knew, but it mattered to him that she had not looked at him with horror drenching those lovely eyes once he'd told her his story. It mattered to him that she'd sought to defend him instead.

He could not for the life of him understand why it *mattered*.

Why she did.

Only that she had from the start. That she made him believe he could have a different sort of ending than the one he was certain he deserved.

"I'm honored," she said quietly now, like nothing so much as another promise, one more solemn vow, and then she kissed him.

She was as sweet as she was enticing, and he drank her in. He let her explore him, tasting him and teasing him, kissing him again and again until he could feel the catch in her breath.

And then, when he couldn't take it any longer, he slid his hands deep into her hair, he hauled her against him and he took control.

If the tent had ignited around them, he wouldn't have noticed.

He simply lifted her to him so that she wrapped her long legs around his hips and her arms around his neck, and still he plundered her mouth. He angled his jaw and he took the kiss deeper, kissing her as if his life depended on it. As if he could kiss her forever. As if time had stopped for precisely this.

And then, when she was making those wild little sounds in the back of her throat that were more precious to him than all the jewels in his possession, in the whole of his treasury and all of his museums besides, he carried her over to the bed and laid her down on the soft cloud of linens.

He stretched out above her, pressing her deeper into the bed and taking her mouth again. And he kept on kissing her. He could not seem to taste her enough. He could not seem to slake his own thirst.

Her hands moved all over him as if she was learning him with her fingertips, soaking him in. He shifted, slipping a hand down to cup the sweet heat of her in his palm. He held her there until she moaned, and only then did he move, slipping beneath the lacy underthings she wore and thrusting his fingers deep into her molten core.

It was his name she cried when she shook around him, and Kavian hoarded that to him like another vow. Her voice against the night, brighter than the lanterns that lit the space around them, etched deep inside him like letters carved into the stone of his own heart.

He was filled then with a kind of wild desperation he'd never felt before. He needed to be inside her, or die of it, and he hardly knew what to make of it when he saw his hands shook slightly as he rid her of her little slip and those lacy panties she wore, then peeled off his own boxer briefs.

Nothing mattered but that slick initial thrust, so deep inside her they seemed more like one, and even that was not enough.

It will never be enough, a voice within him whispered.

And just then, he didn't care.

He gathered her close. His arms wrapped around her,

her mouth against his neck. And he rocked into her, slow and easy. A pace he kept even when she started to shift, to writhe. To move her own hips against his, trying to buck at him and make him go faster.

He laughed, a dark jubilation that seemed to come from every part of him, while she dug her fingers so hard into the skin of his back that he could feel her nails.

And still he held that torturous pace. A slow thrust in, a long drag back. Again and again, driving them both insane.

"Please," she began to whisper. "Please, Kavian. *Please.*"

She was flushed red. Her whole body went stiff and she threw her head back, and Kavian had never seen anything so beautiful in all his life. He pounded into her, his own promise and his own solemn vow, over and over, like a prayer.

And when she burst into flame again, white-hot and endless, she took him with her.

The ride back across the hot sands was different.

Everything is different, Amaya thought.

She sat between Kavian's legs again, with all his lean strength and male heat wrapped around her, hard against her back as the sleek Arabian stallion galloped so smoothly south. She couldn't understand the things that moved in her without name, making her feel as if she hardly knew herself any longer.

The desert stretched out before them and around them, shimmering in the heat, immense and treacherous. Amaya had always hated the desert. The stifling heat. The sheer barrenness and lack of life. The profound emptiness. Its inescapable presence, vast and creeping closer all the time…

Yet that was not at all what she felt today. She wanted the desert to go on forever, vast and unknowable, as immense and beckoning as the sea. Or maybe it was this trip that she wanted never to end. And she had no earthly idea how to feel about that. About any of it. About what had happened out there between them, making the world itself feel altered around them.

It had something to do with how Kavian had woken her that morning, lifting her into his arms and then settling them both into a great tub she hadn't seen the night before, tucked away behind a screen in the far reaches of the tent. She'd winced as she tried to move in the warm, fragrant water, and he'd made a low, rumbling sound that had not quite been a growl.

"Behave," he'd ordered her. "You must let your muscles soak or you will find the ride back sheer agony."

And she'd tried to behave. Truly she had.

But he'd been so hot and hard behind her, his strong arms so perfectly carved as they'd stretched out along the high sides of the bath. The hardest part of him had been like steel, pressed tight against her behind. She'd only shifted position once. Then twice, without really meaning it. Then again, to test the little thrill that had washed through her, before he'd let out a sound that had been something between a laugh and a curse. Both, perhaps. His big hands had gripped her around the waist and he'd lifted her up before settling her on him again, but this time he thrust hard and deep inside her while he did it.

He'd angled them both back again into their original positions, so she'd been lying sprawled over his chest again, her back to his front. And his hardness buried so deep inside her she almost climaxed from that alone.

And then he'd done nothing.

"Is that better?" he'd asked mildly after a moment, and it had been exquisite, to have him so deep within her and to *feel* his voice like that, a rumble against her spine, the tease in it like a drug. "I plan to sit here and soak myself, Amaya. If you wish to do anything else, you must do so all on your own."

But even as he'd said that, his big hands, even warmer now from the water, moved to cover her breasts, sending a kind of delirious electricity rocketing through her as he cupped them, then brushed his thumbs over the tight peaks.

Amaya had tipped her head back so it had been cradled on his wide, hard shoulder, the urge to poke at him as impossible to ignore as his hardness snug inside of her. "I thought you liked to be in charge. That you insisted upon it. I thought that went with the kingly territory."

"I think I can handle a single bath," he'd assured her in that dark, stirring way that made her stomach flip and her core clench hard against the length of him deep within her. "Do as you like, and we'll test that theory."

So that was what Amaya did.

She'd quickly discovered that he'd severely limited her range of motion—but that maybe that was the point. The delicious challenge of it. She'd moved her hips in a sinuous, rocking motion that had them both breathing hard in only a few strokes, and then she'd given herself over to it. She'd learned the beauty in the sweet, slow slide. The lazy circle, all white-hot sensation and endless pleasure.

And all the while his wicked hands had moved between the tight peaks of her breasts and the hot center of her need, helping her build that fire between them, and pouring his own kind of gas on the flame. Until she hadn't been sure who was in charge and who was simply reveling in the heat between them, or why such a thing should matter.

Until she'd forgotten to care.

She had ridden them both to a slow, hot, shattering finish that she'd been sure had left her completely boneless.

Destroyed inside and out. And she'd been fiercely glad that they hadn't been facing each other, because she was terribly afraid Kavian would have seen too easily all the ways she was ripped wide open. That her vulnerability was written right there across her face.

But she thought he knew, even so.

When it had come time to climb back on the horses and head south toward the palace, she was grateful. It had meant long hours for her to put herself back together before anyone could study the ways she'd fallen apart. Before she had to admit it to herself, how broken she'd become out there. Or, far worse, how much she'd liked it. Hours to hide herself away again, behind a mask she hadn't understood she was wearing until he'd torn it off.

"I've never understood the appeal of the desert," she said now, forgetting to censor herself as the sprawling royal stables came into view before them. Was that relief she felt that this ride—this odd interlude—would soon be over? Or something far more complicated?

"Never?" He made that low sound that was his form of laughter, that she found she craved all the more by the day. "But you are the daughter of a mighty desert king. It is deep in your blood whether you understand it or not. It is your birthright."

"I've never cared much for sand," Amaya said.

"Is this where you try to put up all your walls again, *azizty*?" His mouth was right there at her ear, and his voice was a dark flame that lit her from within, that dark current of amusement ratcheting the heat in her even higher. "How many ways must I take you before you understand that there will be no walls between us? There will be nothing but surrender. It would be better by far if you accepted this now."

"Or perhaps I simply do not care for sand," she said, and

she laughed, then felt his hard muscles tighten all around her in reaction. "Not everything is a conspiracy, Kavian. Some things are simply statements."

"And some statements have consequences." His eyes would be gleaming silver if she could see them, she was sure. "As I have been at some pains to show you."

"Is that what you call it? I rather thought you were putting on a grand show. Hauling me into the harem baths, then off to play queen of the desert tribes with no warning. It's almost as if you don't really want a queen at all, so much as a plaything."

"Surely not having to choose is a benefit of royalty," he said, and there was no denying the laughter in his voice then. "I will have to consult the manual upon our return."

Amaya felt that as a victory, the rumble of laughter in his chest behind her. From the man who'd stood before her like marble to tell her the worst of himself, to this man who laughed with her, and it was all her doing. There were darker things that batted at her then, but she ignored them. She would bask in this, even if only for a moment. That she could do this for him. Take a stone and make him a man again. Even if only for a moment.

Even if only for her.

Kavian didn't speak as they rode into the great courtyard. He swung from the horse's back as they entered and led her the rest of the way toward the waiting stable hands. He lifted her from the saddle the way he had before, lowering her to the ground in a manner that only called attention to his superior strength.

And made her wish they were alone so she could feel the drag of his mighty chest against hers again. Like the addict she knew she was.

"We marry in two weeks, Amaya," he said, the vastness of the desert in his voice and silver in his gray eyes, and she felt it like a caress. All of it. His command. His authority. Like a long, hot, drugging kiss. It made her feel alive.

"Perhaps if you didn't keep saying that like it was a dire threat, you'd get a better response," she said, tipping her head back to meet his gaze.

Her reward was that crook of his hard mouth. That gleam in his dark eyes.

"You prefer the threat, I think," he said, and ran a fingertip along the line of her jaw. There was no reason it should echo throughout the rest of her, making even the blood in her veins clamor for more. "You rise to meet it every time. You'll make me an excellent queen, *azizty*."

And when she didn't argue that away for once, when she only met his gaze and let her mouth curve instead, Kavian smiled.

Amaya felt it deep inside her, warm and bright, like a song she told herself she'd let herself sing for a little while.

Just a little while longer.

CHAPTER TEN

WHEN THE WEEK of their wedding dawned, Kavian insisted upon greeting all of their guests in the most formal manner possible, and he didn't much care that the idea of such pomp and circumstance made Amaya balk.

"We're not really going to sit in thrones and wave scepters about, are we?" she asked, her voice as baleful as her gaze as she stared at him from across the length of her dressing room. He'd instructed her attendants to prepare her for court, and the scowl on her face did nothing to take away from the breathtaking new gown she wore or the hair she wore up in a marvelous sweep of combs and braids, exactly as he'd wanted it. She looked exquisite. Deeply, irrevocably regal. The perfect queen.

But Kavian thought he knew this woman well enough by now to know better than to point that out to her. She might have stepped into her role in the desert. But he wasn't fool enough to think she'd accepted it entirely. He needed to marry her, tie her up in legal knots, make sure she understood what he'd known since their betrothal: this was for life. There was no escaping it, for either one of them.

"There is only one throne," he told her mildly. He remained where he was in the doorway as the women fussed over her skirts, his gaze trained on her lovely face and the hint of emotion he could see on her cheeks. "I sit in it. But if you wish to wield a royal scepter, I am certain we can have one made for you."

"Don't be ridiculous." Kavian knew the exact moment she realized that was, perhaps, not the best way to address him in the presence of others. She straightened. Her dark chocolate eyes gleamed with more of that hectic emotion he'd seen more and more of the closer they got to their wedding date. "I don't need a scepter. I have no desire whatsoever to play queen of the castle."

"That is the problem, *azizty*. No one is playing, save you. Because you are, in fact, the queen not only of this particular castle but of all the land."

Her scowl deepened as she dismissed her attendants and walked to him, and he took a moment longer than he should have to admire her. To soak her in. It wasn't merely that she was so beautiful, or how she looked every inch a queen today. It was how perfectly she fit here. In this life. On his arm. At his side.

Did she truly fail to see that? Or was this merely another one of the games she liked to play—her way of teasing him to a distraction? He reached over when she drew near and wrapped his hand around her upper arm, enjoying the way she swallowed. Hard. Because she could deny a thousand things, but never that fire that raged between them. Never that.

"And if you look at me like that in the throne room, in public, in the presence of our guests," he said softly, "you will regret it. I am only as civilized as it suits me to be. That can change in an instant."

She was warm beneath his hand, her skin supple, and he was tempted to ignore the people waiting for them and simply back her up against the nearest wall and—

"You say that as if I do not regret everything already,"

she murmured, but he heard a teasing note in her voice. He could see the sheen of it in her gaze. "Whether you threaten me with it or not."

"I don't make threats, Amaya. I make promises."

She smiled. "And it should worry you, shouldn't it, that one is indistinguishable from the other?"

He dragged his thumb up, then down, enjoying the friction almost as much as the way her lips parted slightly at the sensation. She was his, he thought then, on every possible level. She was surely running out of ways to deny that—and their wedding would put an end to it, once and for all.

But there were miles to go first. Kavian had the suspicion they might be the hardest yet, like any long siege in its final hours. Better to concentrate on the details and assume the rest would fall into place. He reminded himself of the reason he'd come into her dressing room.

"Your mother arrived at the international airport in Ras Kalaat and is en route to the palace," he said, watching her face.

Amaya flinched slightly, so very slightly that had he not been studying her, he might have missed it entirely. She swallowed again, and he saw the pulse in her neck leap, though her face went blank. Panic? Fear? He couldn't tell.

He hated that he still couldn't tell.

"Now?" she asked.

"She will be here in the palace within the hour." He released her arm, straightening in the doorway, frowning down at her. "Were you expecting her? You have gone pale."

"I expected she would attend my wedding, yes," Amaya said. Carefully, he thought. Much too carefully. He was reminded of the mask she'd worn when he'd first met her and it was like a howling thing in him, the urge to tear it off. "I'm her only child, after all, and she is my only remaining parent."

She blinked too hard, then looked around as if she was casting about for an escape route, and it hit him. He'd seen that look on her face before, heard that exact same note in her voice. It had been the night of their betrothal ceremony.

And in the morning, she'd been gone.

"What you did not expect, if I am to read between the lines, was that *this* wedding would ever come to pass," Kavian finished for her. He wanted to touch her again, but didn't, and it hurt like a body blow. "Someday, Amaya, I hope you will come to understand that I keep the promises I make. Always."

She stepped back from him and he felt it like the deepest cut. It took everything he had not to haul her back where she belonged. He watched her pull in a deep breath, as if readying herself for battle.

"It should matter to you that this is not what I want," she said.

It was laughable—and yet Kavian did not feel the least bit like laughing. "You don't know what you want."

"That's astonishingly patronizing. Even for you."

He shrugged, never shifting his gaze from her face. "You ran, I caught you. I will always catch you. That is the end of it."

"It should make a difference that I didn't *want* to be caught," she bit out, as if sobs lurked just there behind her eyes.

"Did you not? It seems to me that if that were the case, you would not have returned to Canada at all, and certainly not to Mont-Tremblant."

Amaya jerked her gaze away from his then, but he didn't stop.

"And, of course, you could have fought me. Showed

me how opposed you were to this union instead of merely making announcements."

"I've done nothing but fight you from the start."

"Yes," he said, and she shivered at his tone. He almost smiled at that. "That is precisely how I would categorize the way you melted in my hands at our betrothal ceremony. And then all over me in that alcove. And then again, how you walked straight into the pools here to join me, wearing almost nothing. What fighting tactics were those, exactly? And to what end?"

She couldn't seem to make herself look at him, but he could see the impact of every word he said. They moved over her, making her tremble, and he'd already confessed his sins. She already knew he was a terrible man. He could not regret this. He did not try.

"You seek my touch and respond to it, always." His voice brooked no argument. It was a statement of flat, inconvertible fact. "Meanwhile, you have not been held here under lock and key or even under special guard. You were left to your own devices out in the desert. You could have made an attempt to leave at any time, yet you have not."

"You would have caught me."

"That is an inevitability, I grant you, but it is a question of where. After all, it took me six months the first time. Yet you have not tried."

"Do you *want* me to make an escape attempt, Kavian?" She turned to glare at him. "Because I thought the point of this was that you wanted a biddable little wife to live out her life at your beck and call."

He felt himself go still.

"That is the first time you have used my name when I have not been touching you, Amaya," he pointed out, and she shuddered. "Who knows? Someday you may even address me as if I am a man with a name, not a strategy to be employed toward your own increasingly convoluted ends."

"Isn't that the point of this?" she asked, and he hardly recognized her voice. "We are nothing but strategies for each other. Cold and calculated. Surely that's the point of an arranged, political marriage."

"You did not have to prove yourself to the villagers out in the northern territory. Where was the calculation there?"

"It was politically savvy on my part, nothing more."

"You could have complained about your treatment here to your brother at any point over these last weeks and caused a major diplomatic incident."

"He is newly married with a small child." She tipped that chin of hers up into the air, because this was what she did. She fought. She never simply surrendered. He admired that most of all, he thought. That indomitable will of hers, like the desert he loved. "He is somewhat busy, I imagine."

"You could have called me a monster when I showed you who I am," he said quietly. She jerked at that, as if he'd hit her. "Others have before you. Will you call the fact that you did not political, too?" He did not let himself think about what he might do if she did. But her eyes were slick with misery and she didn't say a word. "Do you know what it is you want, Amaya? Or do you fear that you already know?"

"None of that means I want to marry you," she whispered.

"Perhaps it does not," he agreed. "But it does suggest that the chances are very good that you will anyway."

"If you remove all the threats from this relationship," she replied now, her voice revealingly thick, "we don't actually have one."

"I will keep that foremost in my thoughts, *azizty*, the next time I am deep inside you and you are begging me for your release." Kavian kept his voice low, because it was the only thing keeping his hands from her, and his court waited for them even now. "I will hold you on that edge until you scream and then I will remind you that we have no relationship. No relationship, no release. Is that what you had in mind?"

He could hear her breathing, too loud and too fast. And her gaze was wild as it met his. But when she spoke, her voice was flat. Almost matter-of-fact.

"They are waiting for us in the throne room," she said.

He didn't believe her apparent calm for a moment. But once again, he admired her courage. The way she stood up to him, the way she gathered herself when he could see the storms in her. The more she kept trying to prove they did not suit, the more perfect he found her.

"They can wait a little while longer." He raised his brows. "Until we arrive, it is only a very large room with a dramatic chair no one is permitted to touch. By law."

"That I get to stand behind, yes," she bit out. She moved then, sweeping past him toward the door, her spine rigid and her head high. "What a joyous experience that will be, I am sure. I can hardly wait."

He let her go, following behind her as she made her way from their suite and into the grand corridor that led toward the public wing of the palace and the ancient throne room that sat at its center. His aides converged upon him as they walked, and it was not until they'd entered the room and taken their places on the raised dais that dominated one end of the ornate hall that he focused on her once more.

"You stand beside me, not behind me," he told her. He could not have said what moved him to do so. That she was still pale. That her sweet mouth was set in a hard line no matter that defiant angle to her fine jaw. That she still seemed to imagine that this was something other than foregone conclusion. "A strong king holds the throne, Amaya, but a strong queen beside him holds the kingdom. So say the poets."

He saw something flicker in her gaze then. "And do you rule with poetry? That doesn't sound like the man who dragged me out of that café in Canada."

"You walked out of that café in Canada of your own volition," he reminded her. "Just as you walked into that encampment in the desert and just as you will walk down that aisle in a few days. My queen obeys me because she chooses it. That is her gift. It is my job to earn it."

An expression he couldn't define moved over her face then, as the guards stood at attention down the length of the long hall and announced the series of guests who awaited their notice, and her mother's arrival. Kavian eyed her as her mother's name rang out, taking in Amaya's too-stiff posture. The way she gripped her hands before her, so hard her knuckles hinted at white.

"You are afraid of your own mother," he murmured. "Why is that?"

But the great doors were opening at the other end of the hall, and she didn't answer him. Because her mother was walking in and Amaya sucked in an audible breath at the sight, as if she couldn't help herself. As if she truly was afraid.

Kavian turned slowly to gaze upon the person who could bring out this reaction in the only woman he'd ever met who had never seemed particularly intimidated by *him*.

Elizaveta al Bakri looked like every photograph Kavian had ever seen of her. She appeared almost supernaturally ageless. She was an icy blonde, her hair swept back into a ruthless chignon and her objectively beautiful face flawless, with only the faintest touch of cosmetics to enhance the high, etched cheekbones she'd passed on to her daughter. Her blue eyes were frigid despite the placid expression on her face, her carriage that of a prima ballerina. She looked tall and willowy and effortless as she strode down the long hall toward the throne, quite as if she hadn't flown halfway across the world today, and yet as far as Kavian was concerned she was little more than a reptile.

Much like his own, long-dead mother.

"Breathe," Kavian ordered Amaya in a dark undertone.

He felt more than saw her stiffen beside him, then he heard her exhale.

He kept his attention on the snake.

Elizaveta made a beautiful, studied obeisance when she came before the throne, sweeping deep into a curtsey and then rising in a single, elegant motion that called attention to her lovely figure. But then, most snakes were mesmerizingly sinuous. That didn't make them any less venomous.

"Your Majesty," Elizaveta murmured, her voice threaded through with the faintest hint of an accent that Kavian suspected she maintained simply to appear slightly exotic wherever she went. Then she shifted her attention to her daughter. "Amaya. Darling. It's been too long."

"You may go to her," Kavian said in an indulgent tone. It was over-the-top even for him and Amaya glanced at him, startled—but he trusted that the look in his eyes was savage enough to keep her from saying anything. Hers widened in response.

Challenge me, he suggested with his gaze alone. *I dare you.*

But Amaya merely moved toward Elizaveta, and Kavian was aware of too many things at once as she went. It was the same overly focused attention to detail that he experienced before an attack, whether while practicing the martial arts he'd trained in all his life or in an actual physical skirmish. The vastness of the great room as it echoed

around his betrothed. The rustle of her long skirts as she
descended the wide stairs. And the way this woman who
was meant to be her mother looked at her as she waited,
her expression still something like serene yet with nothing
but calculation in her chilly gaze as far as he could tell.

The hug was perfunctory, the highly European double-
cheek kiss a performance, and Kavian wanted to throw the
older woman across the room. He wanted her hands *off*
Amaya, that surge of protectiveness coming from deep,
deep inside him, and it took all of his considerable self-
control to keep himself from heeding it.

"I'm so glad you came," Amaya said to her, quietly.

And Kavian reminded himself that this was still her
mother. Amaya actually *meant* that. It was the only reason
he did not throw this creature from his palace.

"Of course I came," Elizaveta replied, bright and
smooth and still. It wedged beneath Kavian's skin like a
blade. "Where else would I be but by your side on your
wedding day?"

"Your maternal instincts are legendary indeed," Kavian
interjected, like a dark fury from above, his gaze the only
thing harder than his voice. "The world is a large place, is
it not, and you have explored so many different corners of
it with Amaya in tow. An unconventional education for a
princess, I am sure."

Elizaveta inclined her head in a show of respect that
Kavian was quite certain was entirely feigned. Amaya
stared back at him, stricken. And he could not hurt her.
He could not.

"But I welcome you to Daar Talaas," he said then, for
the woman who would be his wife. His perfect queen. He
waited for the older woman to raise her head, and then he
nearly smiled. "I do so hope you will enjoy your stay in
my palace. What a shame it will be so brief."

* * *

"He is rather Sturm und Drang, isn't he?" Elizaveta asked Amaya when they were alone hours later, after a long day of formal greetings and diplomatic speeches. She sounded arch and amused and faintly condemning besides. As if this were all a terrific joke but only she knew the punch line. "Even for a sheikh. I'd heard rumors. Is he always *quite* so…commanding?"

Amaya was certain *commanding* was not the word her mother had been about to use just then. They sat in the charming little garden that adjoined Elizaveta's guest suite with hot tea and a selection of sweets laid out before them. Amaya shoved an entire almond pastry into her mouth with a complete lack of decorum, because it was far safer to eat her feelings than share a single one of them with her mother.

"He is the king of Daar Talaas," Amaya replied once she'd swallowed, aware that her mother had probably counted every calorie she'd just consumed and was mentally adding them to Amaya's hips. With prejudice. *She can't help who she became*, she reminded herself sharply. *This isn't her fault. It probably took her more to come here than you can imagine.* "Commanding is simply how he is."

Elizaveta leaned back. She held her tea—black, no sugar, of course—to her lips and sipped, never shifting her cold gaze from Amaya.

"Tell me what you've been up to," Amaya said quickly, because she could practically see the way her mother was coiling up, readying herself to strike the way she always did when she felt anything, and Amaya didn't think she could take it. "We haven't talked in a long time."

"You've been so busy," Elizaveta said, in that light way of hers that wasn't light at all. "Traveling, was it, these last six months? One last hurrah before settling down to this marriage your brother arranged for you?" She didn't quite frown—that would have marred the smoothness of her forehead, and Amaya knew she avoided that at all costs. "I hope you enjoyed yourself. You must know that a man in your betrothed's position will demand you start having children immediately. As many babies as possible, as quickly as possible, to ensure the line of succession. It is your foremost duty."

"There aren't any lines of succession here," Amaya replied, because concentrating on dry facts was far preferable to thinking about other things, like the total lack of birth control she and Kavian had used in all this time. Why hadn't they thought about that? But even as she asked herself the question, she was certain that *he* had. Of course he had. He thought of everything. She trained her gaze on her mother, because she couldn't fall down that rabbit hole. Not now. Not while Elizaveta watched. "Not in the classic sense."

"Every man wants his son to rule the world, Amaya, but none so much as a man who already does." Elizaveta smiled, which only made a chill snake its way down Amaya's back. Had Elizaveta always been so obvious a barracuda? Or was this simply her reaction to being back in this world again—when she'd avoided it all so deliberately since leaving Amaya's father? "You are so very, very young. Are you certain you're ready to be a mother?"

"You were a mother when you were nineteen."

"I was not nearly so sheltered," Elizaveta said dismissively. She shook her head. "I cannot fathom how you could end up in a place like this, with all the advantages I provided you over the years. I had no choice but to marry your father when he appeared like some fairy story to spirit me away. You have nothing but choices and yet here you are. As if you learned nothing."

Amaya should not have felt that like a noose around her throat. It shouldn't have mattered what Elizaveta said. It shouldn't have hit her so hard, right in the gut.

"You told me my father swept you off your feet. That you were in love."

She sounded like the child she had never been, not quite. She couldn't help herself.

"Yes, of course I told you that," her mother replied, arch and amused again. "That sounds so much more romantic than reality, does it not?"

"Anyway," Amaya said tightly, because she didn't believe Elizaveta's sudden nonchalance on this topic after years of wielding her broken heart like a sword, "there's no point having this discussion. I'm twenty-three years old, not nineteen. I'm not even remotely sheltered. And most important, I'm not pregnant."

You can't possibly be pregnant, she told herself ferociously.

Her mother turned that cool blue gaze on her, washed through with something enough like malice to make Amaya's stomach clench. Despite herself, she thought of the things Kavian had said about her. That she had lived off Amaya. That she had lied about that—and who knew what else?

"That's clever, Amaya. Once you are you will be trapped with him forever."

Trapped was not the word that came to mind, which was more than a little startling, but Amaya frowned at her mother instead of investigating that. "Luckily, it's not up to him."

But Elizaveta only smiled again.

Stop making her out to be something scary, Amaya snapped at herself. *She's not a demon. She's nothing but an unhappy woman. This is her hurt talking, not her heart, and anyway, you don't have to respond.*

"Of course not, darling," Elizaveta murmured. She leaned forward and put her teacup back on its saucer with a click that seemed much too loud. "I've never seen you in traditional attire before. Not even when we still lived in Bakri."

Amaya had to order herself to unclench her teeth. To curve her lips in some rendition of a smile. "I am not in traditional attire. You can tell because I am not wearing a veil."

"I wonder if this is merely a stepping stone toward a more traditional arrangement." Elizaveta's shrug was exquisite. It somehow conveyed worry and a kind of jaded weariness at once, while also making her look infinitely delicate. "A sleight of hand, if you will. He lures you in by pretending to be a modern sort of man and then—"

"Mother." It was so absurd she almost laughed. "There is not one thing about Kavian that is the least bit modern. If that's the lure, he's already failed. Spectacularly."

Elizaveta moved to her feet and then wandered with seeming aimlessness around the small courtyard, as if she was taking in all the green and the riot of bright flowers. As if she'd never beheld their like before. "What a charming suite. I adore all these flowers. What part of the palace is this?"

Amaya understood where she was going then. Perhaps it had been inevitable from the start, given how furious her mother had always been at her father. Given how hurt she still clearly was.

"The guest part," she replied. Grudgingly.

Her mother smiled over her shoulder, but her gaze was hard. "Is that its formal name, then? How strange."

She watched her mother trail her always elegant, always red-tipped, always diamond-studded fingers along the petals of the nearest bougainvillea vine.

"I think you know perfectly well that this is technically

part of what was once considered the harem complex," Amaya said quietly. "But Kavian does not keep a harem."

Her mother glanced at her. "Not now, you mean."

"He kept a harem before we met, if that's what you're trying to tell me so subtly." Amaya was proud of how cool she sounded. How very nearly bored, as if the number *seventeen* were not flashing behind her eyes. "But then, he's never claimed to be a monk."

Her mother turned to face her, and Amaya was struck, as she always was, at how much she looked like the darker version of her mother's precise blond beauty. Where Elizaveta was like an ice sculpture, carved to sharp perfection, Amaya was so much softer. Blurrier.

Misshapen, she'd always thought. And yet today she found she was glad they weren't more similar.

"Did he give up his concubines for you?" Elizaveta asked, with that pointed smile that was her fiercest weapon. "That is enough to make the heart sing, I am sure."

Amaya had not spoken to her mother much in the six months she was on the run. There had been enough speculation in the papers that Amaya assumed Elizaveta had guessed that her daughter had run away from an arranged marriage, but Amaya had never confirmed it. Now she was happy she'd played it that way. That she'd confided nothing. That Elizaveta knew nothing at all about Kavian, or Amaya's relationship with him.

"Kavian is deeply romantic," she told her mother, giving her all to that lie. "He might not show it to you or the world. But he is a hard man who has only one bit of softness, and that's me."

Her heart skipped a beat at that, as if it was true. More— as if she wanted it to be true.

But her mother's cold eyes gleamed. "Is that what he told you?"

"I wouldn't put much stock in it if he'd *told* me," Amaya said, and even smiled. "I've learned one or two things from you, I hope. Actions speak louder than words, isn't that what you always said?"

"And when you are big and fat and ugly with his child, as you will be often," Elizaveta said, as if she was agreeing, "you must anticipate that he will see to his needs as he pleases, with as many other women as take his fancy. Men always do. That is their favorite course of action, Amaya. Always. Especially men like him, in places like this."

Amaya rose to her feet and skimmed her hands down her skirts, angling her head high. She wasn't eleven. She didn't have to listen to this. She certainly didn't have to believe it.

"I'm sorry if that was your experience, Mother," she said quietly. "It won't be mine."

And she hadn't understood until she said it out loud that she wanted that to be true. That more of her wanted to believe in Kavian than didn't.

She had no idea what to do with that.

"Does he love you, then?" Elizaveta asked, her voice so light. So terrible. "Or has he merely claimed you?"

Whatever she saw on Amaya's face then made her cluck in what sounded like sympathy. It washed over Amaya like something far more acidic, and wrenched at her heart besides.

"Darling." Elizaveta shook her head, and Amaya felt everything inside turn to ice. "They're not at all the same thing. And a woman must always know where she stands, or she will spend her life on her knees."

CHAPTER ELEVEN

KAVIAN KNEW THE MOMENT Amaya walked into their rooms as the afternoon edged toward evening that her mother had gotten to her. He could hear it in the heaviness in her step out in the foyer. The particular weight of her silence.

The pen he'd forgotten he was holding snapped in his hand and he muttered a curse, throwing the pieces into the wastebasket that sat beside his desk in his private office, the pen fragments making an oddly satisfying sound as they hit the metal sides.

He wished it was the poisonous Elizaveta instead.

"You are not truly planning to sneak past me, are you?" he gritted out, as if to the walls around him. As if to the ghosts that the locals claimed had plagued this place for centuries. "Do you imagine that is wise?"

A moment later, Amaya appeared in the doorway. She was still wearing the gown she'd had on in the throne room earlier, which displayed her femininity so beautifully and yet with such exquisite restraint that it made his throat hurt. That hair of hers that he was beginning to view as an addiction he might well succumb to completely was still caught up in all the braids and twists that he thought made her look something like ethereal. Something so much more than merely a bartered bride, his for the taking, though she was that, too. She was everything.

She was so lovely—so very much Amaya and *his*—it made his chest feel hollow. Scraped raw.

But it took her too long to raise her gaze to his and when she did, those chocolate eyes of hers were much too dark. Too troubled by far. He eyed her from across the span of the room, temper beginning to pound through him as if he were running flat out across the desert sands, straight on toward the enemy.

Amaya crossed her arms over her chest and he hated it. He hated the defensive gesture itself. He hated that she felt she had to make it. Even after he'd combed the whole of the earth for her. Even after everything he'd told her. Even though she knew the truth about him and it had not made her hate him.

Apparently only her mother could do that.

He wanted to throw back his head and howl, like some kind of wild thing, all claws and fangs.

"Why are you looking at me like that?" Amaya's voice was a scrape against the quiet and did very little to calm him.

"How am I looking at you?" he asked. Mildly. "As if I think you might be rationalizing a new way to betray me even as we stand here?" He studied her. "Are you?"

Something sparked in her dark eyes. "I can't betray you, Kavian. By definition. First I would have to pledge myself to you in some meaningful way, of my own volition."

"Careful, Amaya." His voice was rougher, deeper. "Be very, very careful."

The elegant column of her throat moved as she swallowed, but she didn't look away.

"Did you sleep with all seventeen of the women you kept here in your harem?"

He muttered something harsh in Arabic that he was quite certain she understood, but she only tipped that sweet chin of hers higher and let that mouth of hers go mulish. "It's a simple yes or no question."

"Ten of my so-called concubines were under the age of fifteen," he told her, and it was a remarkable experience for him. He had never explained himself to another living soul, as far as he could remember. He had never felt the slightest compulsion to do so. "They were gifts from each of the ten tribes who live in the great desert, as is tradition. I brought them here to educate them, to make them aristocratic women who could do as they pleased rather than chattel to be bartered and traded in the desert encampments. Most of them are currently studying abroad, or have made excellent marriages." He tried not to grit his teeth. "And, no, I did not sleep with these teenagers, Amaya. My tastes run to grown women, as you should know better than anyone."

She didn't crack. "Seven women, then."

"My predecessor kept a number of women. When I got rid of him I sent those with children to the far reaches of the desert, as I could not allow them to remain under my roof. It makes me look weak in the eyes of many of my subjects. Soft in ways that could hurt me." He shrugged. "As long as they dedicate themselves to living quiet lives free of political intrigue, they may do so safe from my interference."

"You mean, as long as they don't show signs of trying to wreak the sort of vengeance you did, you'll let them live."

He didn't back down. "Yes." He let his brows rise. "Does this offend you, Amaya? I have told you. Daar Talaas is not Canada. You may cringe from our brand of justice all you like, but that doesn't make it any less effective."

"I didn't cringe." She shifted. Swallowed again, as if against a lump in her throat. "But that doesn't mean I necessarily support it, either."

"Two of my predecessor's concubines remained in the palace after I took it back," Kavian told her. "But I never touched them. I merely allowed them to stay here after he was gone, as they had no families to take them in. It was widely considered an act of mercy."

She stared at him for a long while. Kavian felt a muscle in his jaw clench tight. His entire body tensed, as if he was moments away from launching an attack. Or perhaps warding one off.

"And of the five other women you kept here?"

He shook his head. "I am a king, Amaya. Should I have *dated* instead? I hear it is fashionable to do so online these days. Perhaps that would have worked. I could have put up an ad, I am sure. *Single sheikh seeks companion for sex on command, no possibility of marriage, yet many financial and residential perks.*" His voice was like acid. "I'm certain the tabloids would have loved that. They are so fond of me already."

Her gaze was hot and level at once. "And of the five—"

"I am not answering any further questions about the harem I disbanded when you asked me to do so. When I promised you I would, because of the two of us, I am the one who keeps promises." He watched her flinch at that, but he couldn't seem to modify his tone at all. "The harem I did without for six months while you led me on a merry chase across the planet. Do you truly wish to discuss this, Amaya?"

There was a glitter in her dark eyes he didn't particularly like. She stood tall and inescapably regal there in the door. "We haven't used birth control of any kind."

"No." He didn't avert his gaze from hers. "We have not."

"Is that how this works, Kavian? You think if you get me pregnant I'll be forced to stay here?"

He heard something far more ragged in her voice then, could see the echo of it in that storm in her too-dark eyes.

"Have I made my intentions unclear?" He studied her face then, wondering at that raw thing inside him. It seemed to grow larger by the moment. "Have I deceived you in some way? Is this what your mother came here to tell you?"

"Don't blame her. She's supposed to look out for me."

"Can you truly claim that was her goal?" He was incredulous.

But Amaya stared at him, openly defiant. "You took advantage—"

"Of your inexperience? Are we acknowledging that now? And I had grown so accustomed to the Whore of Montreal."

"You knew I was inexperienced. You knew I wasn't paying attention to the things I should have been. You used that against me." Her voice didn't shake. Her hands weren't in visible fists. And yet there was a certain sheen to her dark gaze that suggested both. "You want to keep me here against my will, no matter what it takes. Sex around the clock until I can't see straight. Barefoot and pregnant for the next ten years. Whatever works."

"Please remind me, Amaya, of any moment in all the time that you have known me when I indicated otherwise."

Kavian heard his own voice then, so rough and dark in the quiet room, he might as well have kicked down the walls. He was certain he could *see* the way it slammed into her. He saw the way she gulped in a breath. He even saw the way she adjusted her stance, as if her knees had suddenly weakened beneath her.

He didn't recognize the feeling that moved in him then. Thick, dark. A rich thread of an agony he could not name, balling in his gut and sitting there like a stone.

Shame, he realized after a stunned moment. And something like a keening hatred of himself and these battleground tactics on this woman who was no desert warrior, no matter how tough she appeared at times. He'd never felt anything like it.

He didn't much care to experience it now. He moved toward her, aware on some level that his careful veneers were cracking as he moved, the masks he wore shattering—

But he couldn't stop.

"And what will happen when you get what you think you want?" she threw at him, all the tears she was not crying audible in the thickness of her voice, and he hated himself more. "What happens when I give you everything I have and the thrill is gone? When you use me up and cast me aside? Will you consider that an act of mercy, too?"

"You should not listen to the rantings of a bitter old woman. I am not your father."

Her eyes swept over him, that bittersweet shine. "Are you sure about that? Because so far, the two of you seem very much the same."

He felt unchained then. Untamed. Wild beyond measure. And it did not occur to him to temper it at all as he moved toward her.

Kavian didn't stop until he was upon her, right there, looming over her until she stepped back and came up hard against the doorjamb.

"Do you want me to apologize, *azizty*?" It was a growl from the deepest part of him. "In this fantasy of yours, do I beg your forgiveness?"

"You wouldn't mean a word of it even if it was a fantasy."

He stroked the tender skin of her elegant neck, trailing his fingers over her satiny flesh and the tumult of her pulse. He felt the way she trembled, and he saw arousal edge into that darkness in her gaze, whether she wanted it—him—or not.

"No," he agreed, despite those too-dark things that still moved in him. "I would not."

"Kavian."

He knew what she was going to say. He could see the words form on her lips, see them scroll across her face.

"My mother—"

"I will have that snake of a woman removed from the palace within the hour. She—"

"She is my *mother*." Her voice was a shocked whisper.

"Do you think I cannot tell a bad mother when I see one? Can you have forgotten mine? Your mother is a viper. I want her and her poison gone from here."

"No." Amaya's voice was flat. Incredibly bold, for someone so much smaller than he was, so much more fragile, but she stared back at him as if she was unaware of those things. As if she was his equal in every way. As if she had every intention of engaging him in hand-to-hand combat if he didn't do as she asked.

As she commanded.

"I beg your pardon?"

"You heard me." Her chin rose fractionally. "You cannot throw my mother out because you don't like her. I don't *care* if you don't like her."

"*You* do not like her."

She frowned at him. "I love her."

"I cannot abide her." He felt that stone in him, dragging down, threatening his ability to stand before her. Threatening far more than that. "She is envious of you. She whispers poison into your ears. You fear her."

"I feel sorry for her." Her voice was even. Her chest rose and fell too quickly, he thought, and still she smelled of honey and rain and he wanted nothing as much as he wanted her. Nothing at all. "She was hurt a very long time ago, and hurt is what she knows. She can't help the way she lashes out."

He shifted, feeling his mouth flatten as he traced unknowable symbols along the elegant line of her neck, feeling the way she shuddered at his touch. "She is a grown woman who has spent the bulk of her life manipulating others to do her bidding. I do not dance to the tune of fools. Why should I suffer her presence here?"

He saw too many emotions chase each other across her face then, one after the next, and he felt them all like blows.

When she spoke, her voice was quiet. "Because I asked you to."

Kavian shook his head, a harsh negation that had more to do with the memory of Elizaveta's cold gaze, so much like the photographs he'd seen of his weak, vain, treacherous mother.

"Then you can't give me what I want. You can't *give* at all." She raised one shoulder, then dropped it, and he understood that she was not in the least afraid of him. Was that what roared in him, so much like desire? Like greedy admiration? "Don't claim you want a queen to stand beside you, Kavian, when what you really want is your own way in all things."

"I want exactly what I claimed from the start." His voice was practically a growl. "I am exactly who I have always been. More than that, *azizty*, I am exactly who you need."

"Then prove that. I've told you what I need." Her dark eyes searched his face. "I don't need you to understand, Kavian. I need to you listen to me for once."

He didn't recognize the thing that swelled in him then. He didn't understand why he felt as if he'd staggered blindly into a sandstorm and was being tossed this way and that. He only saw something unbreakable in her gaze. Tempered steel, forged in flames.

"If it is what you want," he said stiffly, because words of acquiescence were foreign to him and came slowly, thickly, "she can remain. She is your mother, as you say."

Amaya's eyes glittered. He felt that like another blow, and then her hand came up and slid over his jaw. He felt that touch everywhere. His toes. His sex. His throat.

"Thank you," she whispered, as if he'd given her a kingdom. All the jewels in his possession. "Thank you, Kavian."

That stone thing in him sank deeper. Grew harder. And he hated it all the more.

Kavian was finished talking. He hooked a hand around her neck and jerked her to him, noting with a fierce surge of satisfaction that her nipples were already stiff when they came into contact with his chest.

And then he bent his head and devoured her.

He kissed her with all the roughness within him. That wild thing that battered at him. That uncivilized creature that would have locked her away if it could have, that still thought it might. That great stone, that vast weight, that exploded into hunger the more he tasted of her. The man he could not be for her burst from him and into that kiss. He took her mouth like a storm, a great dark invasion, holding nothing back—

And she met him.

More than met him.

It was wild. Raw. Elemental.

He didn't know if she tore his clothing or he did. He knew he ripped open the bodice of her gown to get at her breasts, to worship them. He knew he sank his hands in the concoction of her hair, the great glory of it.

And God, the taste of her. It blocked out the world.

Then they were down on the floor, right there in his office, rolling and tearing at each other and wild. A hunger unlike any other roared in him, and in her, too. He could feel it as well as his own intense passion.

He thrust into her with more need than finesse. She screamed out his name, and he dug his fists into the thick rug beneath them, holding himself still while she clenched and shook around him and rode out her pleasure, her fingers digging hard into his back.

"Thank you," she whispered again, like the blessing he didn't deserve.

And that was when Kavian began to move.

The banquet the night before the wedding that was being fancifully billed in all the papers as East Meets West at Last—a rather theatrical name for what was, at the end of the day, a rehearsal dinner—seemed to drag on forever, Amaya thought. Dignitaries and aristocrats, many of whom had come in days before, lined the tables in the vast ballroom. A band played. Servants outdid themselves, a brace of belly dancers performed during one of the early courses and Kavian lounged there at the head of the high table with his slate-gray eyes fixed on her as if he expected her to bolt at any moment.

As if he could read her mind, even as she smiled and laughed and played her part for the assembled throng.

The meal ended after what seemed like several excruciating lifetimes and the worst part was, Amaya thought as she stood and dispensed her thanks to the guests, this was all her fault. There was something wrong inside her. Twisted. *Not right*. There was no other explanation. How else could she come to terms with the fact that she simply could not resist this man? Because if she'd had any kind of backbone, as he'd pointed out to her himself, she'd have attempted to escape him. She'd have done it, come to that. And she wouldn't have found herself standing here, poised to do the only thing worse than what she'd done to him six months back.

"Are you ready for tomorrow?" Her mother's voice sliced into her, but Amaya only smiled harder, hoping no one was paying too close attention as the crowd moved from the tables to the great room beyond, where desserts were to be passed instead of served, the better for the politicians to wield their trade as they moved from group to group.

Was she ready? How could Amaya still not know?

"Yes," she said, because she didn't want to second-guess herself. She didn't want to keep ripping herself apart.

"It's the right thing, darling. You'll see." But what Amaya heard was that thread of triumph in her mother's voice. That hint of smugness. "Men like him can only be the way they are. It never changes."

"Mother." She had to check her tone, remind herself where they were. "You don't actually know him. You know his title."

"I know men."

"You know what you want to know, and nothing more." Amaya glanced around, afraid someone might have overheard that tense tone in her voice, but most of the guests had moved toward the other side of the great hall and on toward the waiting courtyard. She and Elizaveta were as alone as it was possible to be in such a great crowd.

Her mother's gaze was as cool as her smile was polished. "I don't know what you mean, Amaya."

"It doesn't matter." Amaya's smile felt welded to her face. "This isn't the place to discuss it."

They would have all their lonely lives for that, she thought—and she felt hollow. Utterly empty and dark. But that was to be expected. She wouldn't be leaving Daar

Talaas unscathed. She'd be surprised if she even recognized herself.

"I don't think I care for your tone of voice," Elizabeta replied, her tone light. But her blue eyes were hard. "Is that the kind of disrespect you learned here? We can't get you away from him fast enough."

"Did we live off a trust my father set up for me when I was a child?" Amaya hadn't known she meant to fire that at her mother until she did it. And when Elizaveta froze, she wanted to grab the words back—except instead, she continued. "Is that how we survived those years? Because I must have misunderstood. I thought you told me we had to move around so much because we were destitute."

She saw the truth in her mother's face, so much like her own. She saw the glitter of it in her mother's gaze.

"Things were a good deal more complicated than you can possibly understand," Elizaveta said, her voice chilly in the warm room.

"That's all right, Mother." It wasn't until she spoke that Amaya heard the bitter edge to her words. That she felt it inside her, spiked and painful. "Lucky for you, I'm far more forgiving than you are."

She started to move away then, her emotions blinding her and her breath much too ragged, but her mother's hand on her arm stopped her.

"It's not forgiveness," Elizaveta said crisply. "It's weakness. Haven't I taught you the difference? Your trouble is, you make yourself a doormat for anyone who happens by and wishes to wipe their feet on you. That's the difference between us."

Something cracked then, so loud and so huge that Amaya was surprised she didn't hear screams from the crowd. It took her a stunned moment to understand that the palace hadn't crashed down around them—that something had instead toppled over inside her. She could feel the aftershocks, shaking through her.

She reached down and tugged her mother's elegant hand from her arm.

"I choose how I bend, Mother," she said. She might have shouted it, though she knew she hadn't—yet she saw the dazed look in Elizaveta's eyes as if she had. Amaya could only wonder what expression was on her face. She found she couldn't bring herself to care. "And to whom. I only kneel when I want to kneel, and that doesn't make me a doormat. I've spent my life catering to you because I love you, not because I'm weaker than you. You've spent your life prostrate to your feelings for a man who forgot you the moment you left him, if not long before, because you were never as strong as you pretended to be. That's the difference between you and me. I'm not pretending."

"You must be crazy if you think a man like Kavian thinks of you as anything but a conquest," Elizaveta hissed.

"Don't mention him again," Amaya said, with a certain finality that she could see made her unflappable mother blink. "Not ever again. He is off-limits to you. As am I."

"I am your mother!" Elizaveta huffed at her, as if Amaya had punched her.

"And I love you," Amaya said with a certain fierce serenity that reminded her of Kavian's desert. "I always will. But if you can't treat me with respect, you won't see me again. It's that simple."

For the first time in as long as she could recall, her mother looked old. Something like frail. But Amaya only gazed at her, and ignored the pity that made her heart clench tight.

"Amaya."

"This isn't a debate," she said quietly. "It's a fact."

She left her mother standing there, looking lost, for the

first time in her memory. It took a few steps to remember herself. To smile. To incline her head as regally as possible as she caught the eye of this or that noble personage. Amaya moved through the crowd as she reached the waiting courtyard, open to the night sky above with a series of decorative pools and fountains marking its center.

Kavian stood on the far side of the pools, that stark, harsh face of his intent as he listened to the two Daar Talaasian generals before him. As if he'd sensed her approach, or her eyes on him, his gaze snapped to hers across the night.

And for a moment there was nothing but that. Nothing but them. No crowd, no guests. No wedding in the morning.

His face was as brutally captivating as ever, and she knew it so much better now. She felt him deep inside her, as if he'd wrapped himself around her bones, taken her air. She felt him as if he was standing beside her instead of across a grand courtyard, as if they were alone instead of surrounded by so many people.

She thought she might feel him like this, as if they'd fused together somehow on some kind of molecular level, all the rest of the days of her life. Amaya told herself that what moved in her then, thick and harsh, was not grief. It couldn't have been.

"You do not look the part of the blushing bride to be, little sister."

Amaya started at the familiar voice at her ear, then controlled herself, jerked her attention away from Kavian and aimed her practiced smile at her brother.

But Rihad, king of Bakri, did not smile in return. His dark eyes probed hers, and Amaya had to look away, back to where the man who had scandalously kidnapped her from a café in a Canadian lake town stood there so calmly, as if he'd had every right to do so. Quite as if there weren't reporters everywhere, recording every moment of this night for posterity and dramatic headline potential, who wouldn't leap at that story if she'd chosen to share it.

If you marry him, scandals like that will seem like mountains made out of molehills, a small voice within told her. *If you do not, they will take over two countries and drown them both...*

She knew what she had to do if she wanted to survive. She'd set everything in motion. But that didn't make any of it easy. She cared a great deal more about what would happen in the wake of this decision than she had half a year ago.

Obviously. Or she wouldn't still be here.

"You look something very much like happy these days, Rihad," she said after a moment, "I don't think I realized that was a possibility."

For him. For her. For any of them.

He frowned. "Amaya."

But she refused to do this. She *couldn't* do this—and she'd already revealed too much. There was too much at stake.

"Not here, please." She forced another smile. "I will no doubt burst into tears at all your brotherly concern and it will cause a war, and I'll forever be known as that selfish, emotionally overwrought princess who caused so much trouble. There's a reason Helen of Troy doesn't have the greatest reputation. It's not worth it."

"Listen to me," Rihad commanded her, in that voice of his that reminded her that he was not only her older brother. He was a king. Her king.

Amaya remembered his own wedding to his first wife, which had come at the end of a week of celebrations in Bakri City. That, too, had been arranged. Amaya had been a small girl, in awe. She'd thought the fact of the wedding itself meant the bride and groom had loved each other. And in truth, Rihad had always told her that he and his first wife had gotten along well.

But it was nothing next to what was between him and Sterling, his second wife. That much had been obvious at a glance when they arrived the day before. Their connection crackled from the many tabloid articles that had been written about them, which in turn paled next to the sparks they struck off each other in person. Amaya didn't pretend to understand how that could be, when Sterling had spent a decade as their late brother, Omar's, mistress.

She only knew that she and Kavian didn't have the same thing. What they had was dark and physical. A terrible wanting that she was absolutely certain would destroy them both. It was not the calm affection of Rihad's first union. Nor was it the obvious intimacy of his second.

It was an agony.

"It will not be pretty if you fail to go through with this wedding," Rihad said in a gruff sort of voice. "I can't deny that. But I won't force you to the altar. I do not care what claim he thinks he has."

Amaya looked across the great courtyard to find Kavian again, and again his dark gaze met hers, so gray. So knowing. So fierce and hard at once, searing straight into her like a touch of his warrior's hands.

And she understood then.

It was the night before the wedding she'd been trying to avoid for more than six months. And Amaya was deeply and madly and incontrovertibly in love with the man she was meant to marry in the morning. She thought she had been since the moment they met, when those slate-gray eyes of his, so dark and so patient, had met hers and held.

Shifting everything else.

Changing the whole world.

She loved him. She understood with a certain fatalism, a shuddering slide that seemed to have no end inside her, that she always would.

And if she married him, she would become her mother. It was a one-way ticket to Elizaveta's sad life, no matter what Amaya might have told her earlier. If Amaya had Kavian's children, would she treat them the same way Elizaveta had treated her? Once he tired of her and cast her aside, would she spend the rest of her days wandering from lover to lover, playing out the same sort of vicious games and making everyone who came near her as unhappy and bitter as she was?

There were fates worse than death, Amaya thought then, her head thick and dizzy with this knowledge she didn't want. And that was one of them.

"Are you all right?" Rihad asked, the beginnings of a frown between his brows. "Amaya?"

She would never know how she managed to smile at her brother then, when inside her, everything was a great storm. There were no foundations left. She loved Kavian and she couldn't have him and all was ash. Ash and grief and a terrible darkness that scarred her even as it burrowed deep. Because he'd showed her who he was. How he was made. He'd showed her how much he could bend already—and it was so little. Too little.

What would happen when he no longer bothered to try?

"Don't be silly," she said to her brother, the king of Bakri like their father before him. The ruler who had traded her to this man she'd never escape, not really, not intact. She was already in pieces. She understood she would never really be anything else.

When she betrayed Rihad, Rihad and Kavian and two kingdoms between them, she imagined she would shatter even more. Turn to dust out there somewhere on that same lonely circuit, making history repeat itself in her mother's bitter wake.

And that was still better than staying with Kavian and loving him until it killed something in her. Better to love a brick wall, she thought miserably. It was far more likely to love her back.

But here, now, she widened her smile and tried to look as if she meant it. She thought from Rihad's expression that she almost pulled it off. Almost. "I've never been better in my life."

CHAPTER TWELVE

AMAYA FELT HIM behind her, as though he was a part of the shadows out on the terrace not long before dawn. Darker and more electric.

But she didn't look over her shoulder at him. She kept her eyes trained on the soft lights that spread out in the valley below her, making the old city sparkle in the lingering dark. The great immensity of the mountains rose on the other side of the ancient valley and beyond it, the great desert stretched out in all directions and had taken up some kind of residence in her soul without her knowing it until now.

Up above, the stars waited. A bright smear across what was left of the night, fading away by the moment.

"You're not supposed to be here," she said when she thought she could speak. When she thought she could push the words out around the heaviness that was turning her to concrete inside.

"Because you think I am bound by tradition or because you hoped to be halfway to Istanbul by now?"

Kavian's voice was soft. But so lethal there was no chance whatsoever that she might have missed it.

Still, Amaya took her time facing him. When she did, she had to catch her breath against that instant surge of sensation that almost took her from her feet. She had to reach back behind her and hold on to the railing that kept her from plummeting over the side of the high palace walls.

He was dressed all in black. Again. He looked like some kind of assassin, in the same way he had that day back in Canada that felt like lifetimes ago now. His strong arms were folded over his black T-shirt and he was barefoot beneath his black trousers, and her body shivered into that instant, near-painful awareness that she thought would never leave her. He was as much a part of her as the heart that knocked much too hard against her ribs. More.

"You told me at the party that I could have this one last night alone to—"

"Spare me the lies, Amaya."

She jolted at that. At that harshness in his voice, stamped all over his face.

"I haven't said anything," she heard herself say, as if from afar. "How could I have lied?"

"Did you pack a bag?"

Her throat went dry then. How long had he been watching her tonight? "No."

"You did. Not a suitcase, merely a rucksack, but I think you will agree that is splitting hairs at best."

Her heart was a riot in her chest. "Have you been spying on me, Kavian? The night before our wedding?"

"Our wedding." He let out a little laugh, entirely devoid of humor. "What I cannot figure out is why you are still here. Your mother was so explicit in her instructions to my men, who I believe she thinks she managed to turn against me. You were to sneak out through the palace kitchens. She would have transport ready to take you through the tunnels and spirit you out of my evil clutches at last, the better to humiliate me further in the eyes of the world."

Amaya wanted to die, right where she stood. She felt that dizziness return and with it, all that wet heat behind her eyes she tried desperately to keep at bay.

"I know you might not understand this," she said as best she could. "But she loves me, too, in her way."

The look he gave her should have set her on fire. Amaya felt singed as if it had. She straightened from the terrace and took a step toward him, but stopped when he lifted one of his hard, scarred hands.

"Do not come any closer to me." Dark and brutal.

"Kavian—"

But she couldn't finish. His gray eyes were the darkest she'd ever seen them. The night around them was edging into blue, but his gaze stayed much too black. And for the first time since she'd met this man, there was no glimmer in there. No relief.

"You conspired with a woman who is little better than a cobra to run from me, again, after you prevailed upon me to let her stay here when I wanted her removed," he said, as if he was rendering judgment. "But this time, I was to stand at the Western altar you insisted upon and wait for you. Is this not so?"

"Kavian."

"I do not know what it is you want that I have not given you." His voice was a dark throb then, as much inside her as it was in the air between them. "A kingdom. A throne. *Me.* I do not know what you think you will find out there."

Amaya didn't know when her arms had snuck around her own middle, only that she held herself tight as if, were she to let go, she would fall apart. And still she couldn't look away from him.

"I imagine you must want declarations, poetry. I am not that man. I am brute force poured into an old throne, masquerading as a man. I am not soft. I cannot shine the way others do, perhaps. But I would protect your life before my own. I would worship you all the rest of my days."

"You would keep me here."

"You like it here." He didn't precisely shout that last. He didn't have to. "I watched you for days before we picked you up in that lakeside town. You were miserable."

"I was on the run!" she protested, but she was shaken.

"You were lost and alone," he gritted out at her. "But then, I have met your mother, Amaya. You always were."

She sucked in a breath, and it hurt. All of this hurt. It always had.

"I hate it when you do this," she seethed at him. Maybe at herself. "You don't know anything about me!"

"I know everything about you," he threw back at her, harsh but certain. "That is what I have been trying to tell you. I do not know how to *date*. I am not romantic. But I saw your face, I heard your voice and I altered my world to have you. I have nothing else to give you but that."

"What if I don't want it?"

He moved then. He crossed the terrace like lightning and he hauled her against him, his tough hands wrapped around her biceps, yanking her up on her toes. He put his face directly in hers.

"You have never wanted anything more in your life."

Amaya pushed at him, but he didn't let her go, and the tears she'd tried to keep at bay poured over and ran down her cheeks. And Kavian was like an avenging angel towering over her, forcing her to face the things she most wanted to pretend she didn't see.

"I've told you from the start what I wanted," she threw at him, desperate and wild. Because she loved him, and she knew where that led. She knew who it would make her, what she would become. "Let me go, Kavian. Just let me go!"

She saw something rip across his face, too harsh and too dark to bear, and then he opened up his hands. Impossibly, he released her. She staggered back, catching herself against the railing again, unable to look away from him and unable to catch her breath.

Unable to believe he'd done it.

He was breathing as heavily as if he'd been running, and for a taut, electric moment, that was all there was. That and what was left of her heart.

"I will honor my military commitments to your brother," Kavian said, and for a long beat, then another, Amaya had no idea what he was talking about.

Then she did. And it was as if he'd extinguished the stars that easily.

"Hear me, Amaya," he said in that same voice, all command. All of him a king who had won his throne with the strength of his own hands. And more, the man who had conquered her with a glance six months ago, no matter what lies she'd told herself since. No matter her contortions. Her desperate pretense. "I will not pursue you. I will not come after you."

She couldn't speak. She told herself she should feel relief. She should. She was sure she would start at any moment, once it sank in.

"If you do not have a doctor forward the results of a pregnancy test exactly one month from now, I will send one of my physicians to you and have him administer it. If you are pregnant—"

"I can't be." Her voice hardly sounded like hers. It was too thick, too distorted. *Broken*, she thought. "I can't possibly be."

His eyes glittered in the strange, predawn light.

"Then you have nothing to worry about. I am sure you will find that convenient."

And she realized then that she'd never seen him look at her like this before. So cold. So remote. That he had never before seemed anything but fascinated with her, even when he was wild with rage, with passion.

This was a Kavian she didn't know. And that revelation smashed the remaining pieces of that broken heart of hers into smithereens. Until nothing remained but dust. And regret. And that loneliness she'd always carried deep inside her, like her own bones.

"Do you need me to sign something?" she asked.

He didn't appear to move, or even to breathe. Yet she thought she saw a muscle clench in his lean jaw.

"Why?" His voice was a dark lash. "You signed many things six months ago. Your word, your signature, your promises—these are all meaningless."

She wanted to reach out and touch him, but she didn't dare.

"Kavian—"

"You wanted to go, Amaya." His voice was so harsh it bordered on cruel then. "Go. You do not need to sneak off through the tunnels like a refugee. I will have the helicopter waiting, and the plane. You can take it wherever you wish. Just make certain you also take your mother."

"I thought..." She had no idea what she meant to say and she swayed slightly on her feet as if the ground buckled beneath her. "I thought you wanted..."

"I want you," he bit out. "But I will not force you and I will not play this game any longer, where you pretend that is what I am doing when it is what you want. Go, Amaya. Be free. But remember, I know you. This is the only real home you've ever known. *I* am."

And she knew he was right. Maybe that was why she fought it.

Maybe that was why she was still here. Standing here, almost as if she'd been waiting for him to find her.

Still, she fought. "It's a big world. There are a lot of places out there."

He shook his head. "You've seen them all. You've been dragged everywhere. There are no secrets out there, Amaya. You know them already."

"I don't belong here." She only realized she was whispering, raw and broken, when she saw a hint of that calm gray in his eyes again, edging out that awful blackness. That cold.

"Azizty," he said with absolute certainty, "this is the only place you belong. With me."

"You want my abject and utter surrender. You want me to kneel in front of you. You want me to beg."

"Perhaps," he said simply, "that is because you do, too, after you fight it for a time. You are simply too afraid to accept that we both want this. We both like this. This is what we were born to do, together."

"Kavian—"

But he shook his head, cutting her off.

"The sun is rising," he said. "The day is upon us. You have a decision to make, Amaya. I suggest you make it as quickly as possible. Then go, if you mean to go. I have a wedding to cancel and a terrible scandal to manage."

And then he turned on his heel and walked away from her.

She couldn't believe it. It didn't make any sense. He was not the one who left, she was. She couldn't *breathe*—

And then the desert sun peeked over the far hills, and the golden light bloomed, molten and bright, blinding her as it poured down into the valley. It washed over the palace, wrapped her in its instant warmth, transformed the world.

And Amaya understood, at last.

The lesson of the stars, of that great weight. Of the desert. Of the sun.

All of these things were love.

They did not bend, they simply were. They could not be altered or changed, they were far too immense. They were infinite. What did it matter what her mother said? What did it matter what the world said, for that matter? Or those voices inside her that told her what she *should* feel, not what she *did* feel?

The only thing that had ever mattered was love. And when she looked in Kavian's beautiful gray eyes, she'd always seen that greatness, that eternity, that sheer and shocking boundlessness.

Why *wouldn't* she surrender? Wasn't that the point?

And for a man like Kavian, who had done what he had, who ruled this stark and uncompromising place and had for more than a decade—what had his acquiescence to her on the subject of Elizaveta been if not the equivalent?

Amaya scrambled forward then, flinging herself into the great suite, her feet slippery against the marble floors. He wasn't in their bedroom. He wasn't in the grand shower. She raced down the long hall, frantically checking the salons as she passed, and was almost to the point of hysteria when she found him standing in his office again, a mobile phone in his hand.

She had the distant impression that he looked surprised, but she didn't wait to look any closer. She simply threw herself at him, trusting that he would catch her—

And he did.

He always did.

"I let you go," he said darkly as he set her on her feet,

and she watched him go still again as she kept going, sinking right down to her knees before him. More than that, she felt every single muscle in his body go taut beneath her hands.

"I love you," she said.

And for a long, long time, it seemed, ages and epochs, there was nothing but that arrested look in his eyes and that mad clamor in her chest.

"Yes, *azizty*, I know," he said at last, the arrogant man. "I have been trying to tell you this for some time."

It was better than love poems from another. Far better. And the words rolled out of her then, an unstoppable force, like the brand-new day over those old mountains all around them.

"It doesn't matter if you can't love me back," she assured him. She meant it, with every last part of her. "I don't want to be like my mother. I don't want you to sleep with a whole new harem when I get pregnant, every time I get pregnant. I don't want to share you with anyone. I don't want to disappear in you, bending and bending until there's none of me left." She pulled in a shuddering breath, tears slicking her vision, so he was nothing but a dark, blurry blade there above her. "But if that's the price, I can pay it. I will. Because you're right, Kavian. You're right." She was shaking, and she gripped the material of his trousers in her fists. "This is the only place I belong. With you."

She thought he would laugh then. Order her to remove her clothes so he could surge deep inside her, showing her precisely how they fit. Prove, once again, that he was a man hewn from stone, not flesh.

And she wanted that. She wanted him, however she could have him. There was no shame in that. There was only love.

But instead Kavian breathed in deep, then let it out. Long and hard, as if it hurt.

And then His Royal Highness, Kavian ibn Zayed al Talaas, ruling sheikh of Daar Talaas, sank down on his knees before her.

His mouth crooked in the corner at her thunderstruck expression. And then he reached over and took her face in his hands, cradling her as if she was infinitely precious to him.

"This *is* love," he said, his voice a deep rumble. "This is what it looks like. You haunted me from the moment I saw you. I hunted you across the world. You live in my body, you move in my veins, you are my blood. You are mine." He shook his head, his gray eyes stern, his mouth that unsmiling line she adored. "You will never be like your mother. She loves no one and she never will. You will never have to worry about me betraying you, pregnant or not. I do not share well. I do not expect you to be any more giving in that area than I am. And there is no price to pay, *azizty*." He angled his head closer, brushing his mouth over hers. "There is only this."

He kissed her, and the world was made new. He kissed her, and he loved her, and Amaya felt as large as the desert, as bright as the stars, as golden straight through as the sunlight that danced through the room.

Kavian angled his head away, waiting until she opened her eyes and looked at him. That serious, warrior's face of his, harsh and tough. That hard mouth. Those ruthless gray eyes. He was stark and made of stone, and he was hers. He was all hers. She thought it might take her a lifetime or two to get used to it. At the very least.

"I love you, Amaya," he said, quiet and true. And it sang in her, like a great chorus with no end. His mouth shifted into that little crook that was his smile and lit her up from the inside out. "Marry me."

She smiled and snuck her arms around his neck, moving closer so they were flush against each other, still down on their knees. Together.

"Are you asking me?" she teased him. "Because that sounded a lot like another order. A royal command."

"I am asking you. I doubt such a thing will happen again." He slid one hand up into her hair, the other down to grip her hip, holding her close.

She smiled at him, holding nothing back. Surrendering everything, risking everything, and she'd never felt stronger in all her life. Or more sure.

"Marry me, Amaya." Those gray eyes of his gleamed. "Please."

Terrifying sheikhs did not yield to anything, Amaya thought then, and *this* sheikh least of all. He'd proved that a thousand times.

But it seemed even Kavian could bend.

Just a little.

Just enough.

"I will," she said softly. And she held his gaze, the way she hadn't done when they signed all those papers. The way she hadn't before she ran from him the first time. Because this time, she knew what she was vowing, and she meant every word of it. "I promise you, Kavian. I will."

And then she wound herself around him, pressed her mouth to his and showed him exactly how much she meant it.

Kavian claimed his queen in a grandiose ceremony that was reprinted in a thousand papers all over the world and broadcast on far too many channels to count. Bakri and Daar Talaas, united as one in the eyes of the world and against their common enemies.

His wife, his at last.

"This way," he told her with complete satisfaction when they were bound to each other in three languages, two religious systems and under the laws of at least three countries, "there can be absolutely no mistake. You are mine."

"I am yours," she agreed, with a smile that nearly undid him.

And she was. Finally, she was.

More than that, she was the queen he'd always dreamed she'd be. She was beautiful enough to stand at his side and make the nation sigh in wonder. And she was capable enough to do her good works, dirtying her hands when necessary, making the nation love her as he did. The people admired her as much for leading him on a merry chase as for her eventual surrender, and they called her *the strong queen*, like the old poems, as if they believed she was as much a warrior queen as he was her warrior king.

They loved her.

They loved her even more when she gave him his first son some eight months after their wedding, bringing Kavian's own bloody circle to a far happier conclusion. This son would not need to avenge his father. This son would not need to wonder what kind of man he was—he would know.

And they called for national holidays when Amaya gave him his first daughter a year and a half later, the prettiest little girl in the history of the world—according to the besotted king, who considered making that declaration into law.

Kavian made her the greatest queen in the history of Daar Talaas.

But Amaya made him a man.

She loved him fiercely and fully, and demanded nothing but the same in return. She fought him as passionately as she made love to him, and he learned how to bend. Just a little. Just enough. She forgave him and she redeemed him, every day.

She taught him. Every day, she taught him. He did not have her mother thrown in his prisons as he'd wanted, and he saw the benefit of that as the years passed. Elizaveta would never be warm or cuddly, or even, to his mind, tolerable—but she was a far better grandmother than she had ever been a mother.

"She has softened," he said to Amaya one day. They stood together in the old harem, watching Elizaveta and the children play in the desert sunshine that danced through the courtyard. The blonde woman laughed as she held his squirming five-year-old daughter aloft. When she was with their children, she was unrecognizable. "I would never have believed it."

"She's not the only one who has softened," Amaya said, and only smiled at him when he glared at her in mock outrage.

"I am a man of stone, *azizty,*" he said, but he couldn't keep himself from smiling. Amaya didn't try. She laughed at him instead, and the world stopped. The way it had when he watched a video of her a lifetime ago. The way it would, he was certain, when they were both old and gray and addled.

"You are a man," she agreed, and surged up on her toes to kiss him, hard and sweet and fast. Kavian felt her smile against his mouth, and deep in his heart besides. "My man."

And then she took his hand in hers and led them out into the sun, and all the bright days of their future.

* * * * *

Available September 15, 2015

#3369 CLAIMED FOR MAKAROV'S BABY
The Bond of Billionaires
by Sharon Kendrick

Dimitri Makarov's former secretary, Erin Turner, is getting married. But instead of congratulating the happy couple, the masterful oligarch plans to stop the wedding. Because the blushing bride...is also mother to his secret son!

#3370 AN HEIR FIT FOR A KING
One Night With Consequences
by Abby Green

After entering a Parisian perfume house to buy a fragrance for a current lover, exiled King Alix Saint Croix leaves with a powerful craving for another woman altogether—stunningly exotic perfumer Leila Verughese. But it's an alchemy with life-changing repercussions...

#3371 REUNITED FOR THE BILLIONAIRE'S LEGACY
The Tenacious Tycoons
by Jennifer Hayward

Diana Taylor's marriage to Coburn Grant was short and passionate until the reality of their different worlds set in. Now, years later, Coburn has finally agreed to a divorce. Except one last *pleasurable* night together seals their fate—with a baby!

#3372 THE WEDDING NIGHT DEBT
by Cathy Williams

Billionaire Dio Ruiz's convenient union was meant to secure two things: vengeance and the enticing Lucy Bishop. But then Dio found his marriage bed *in*conveniently empty. Two years later, his virgin bride wants a divorce. But freedom has a price...

#3373 SEDUCING HIS ENEMY'S DAUGHTER
by Annie West

Donato Salazar's plan to jilt his enemy's daughter is the ultimate revenge and beautiful Ella Sanderson is certainly sweet enough! But as their fake wedding day approaches, one question weighs heavily on Donato's mind: to love, honor...and betray?

#3374 HIDDEN IN THE SHEIKH'S HAREM
by Michelle Conder

When Prince Zachim Darkhan escapes capture he takes the daughter of his nemesis with him. But while Farah Hajjar is hidden in his harem the line between hatred and desire soon blurs, leading Zachim past the point of no return.

#3375 THE RETURN OF ANTONIDES
by Anne McAllister

Widow Holly Halloran's fresh start is only a plane ride away, until Lukas Antonides—the man she wishes she could forget—strides arrogantly back into her life. As tension mounts between them, so too does that bubbling attraction of old...

#3376 RESISTING THE SICILIAN PLAYBOY
by Amanda Cinelli

Leo Valente is as notorious as the tabloids say he is. But feisty wedding planner Dara Devlin isn't deterred. She needs his family castle for her top client, so she boldly accepts Leo's outrageous challenge to be his fake girlfriend!

REQUEST YOUR FREE BOOKS!

HARLEQUIN

Presents®

2 FREE NOVELS PLUS
2 FREE GIFTS!

PASSION · SEDUCTION GUARANTEED

YES! Please send me 2 FREE Harlequin Presents® novels and my 2 FREE gifts (gifts are worth about $10). After receiving them, if I don't wish to receive any more books, I can return the shipping statement marked "cancel." If I don't cancel, I will receive 6 brand-new novels every month and be billed just $4.30 per book in the U.S. or $5.24 per book in Canada. That's a saving of at least 13% off the cover price! It's quite a bargain! Shipping and handling is just 50¢ per book in the U.S. and 75¢ per book in Canada.* I understand that accepting the 2 free books and gifts places me under no obligation to buy anything. I can always return a shipment and cancel at any time. Even if I never buy another book, the two free books and gifts are mine to keep forever.

106/306 HDN GHRP

Name	(PLEASE PRINT)

Address	Apt. #

City	State/Prov.	Zip/Postal Code

Signature (if under 18, a parent or guardian must sign)

Mail to the **Reader Service:**
IN U.S.A.: P.O. Box 1867, Buffalo, NY 14240-1867
IN CANADA: P.O. Box 609, Fort Erie, Ontario L2A 5X3

**Are you a current subscriber to Harlequin Presents® books
and want to receive the larger-print edition?
Call 1-800-873-8635 or visit www.ReaderService.com.**

* Terms and prices subject to change without notice. Prices do not include applicable taxes. Sales tax applicable in N.Y. Canadian residents will be charged applicable taxes. Offer not valid in Quebec. This offer is limited to one order per household. Not valid for current subscribers to Harlequin Presents® books. All orders subject to credit approval. Credit or debit balances in a customer's account(s) may be offset by any other outstanding balance owed by or to the customer. Please allow 4 to 6 weeks for delivery. Offer available while quantities last.

HP15

"Are you asking me to pose as your date?"

"What other reason would we have for being in Palermo together? I think it's the most believable scenario, don't you?"

Maybe it was tiredness after the past twenty-four hours catching up with her, but Dara felt a wave of hysterical laughter threatening to bubble up to the surface. The thought that anyone would believe a man like Leo Valente was dating a plain Irish nobody like her was absolutely ludicrous.

He continued, oblivious to her stunned reaction. "You would leave the business talk to me. All I'd need is for you to act as a buffer of sorts—play on your history with his family. Someone with a personal connection to smooth the way."

"A buffer? That sounds so flattering…" she muttered.

"You would get all the benefits of being my companion, being a guest at an exclusive event. It would be enjoyable, I believe."

"Umberto Lucchesi is a powerful man. He must have good reason not to trust you," she mused. "I'm not quite sure I can risk my reputation."

"I'm a powerful man, Dara. You climbed up a building to get a meeting with me. I'm offering you an opportunity to get exactly what you want. It's up to you if you take it or not."

The limo came to a stop. Dara looked out at the hotel's dull gray exterior, trying desperately to get a handle on the situation. He was essentially offering her the *castello* on a silver platter. All she had to do was play a part until he got his meeting and she would be done.

"What happens if you're wrong? If having a buffer makes no difference?"

"Let me worry about that. My offer is simple. Come with me to Palermo and I will sign your event contract for the castle."

She thought about the risk of trusting him. He hadn't given her any reason to trust him so far. But what other possible reason could he have for asking her to go with him?

A man like him could have any woman he wanted, so it wasn't simply attraction—she was sure of that.

He obviously wanted in on the Lucchesi deal very badly if it had prompted him to consider her event. His reaction earlier had been a complete contrast, his refusal so clear. It was a risk to lie to a man like Umberto Lucchesi, but on the scale of things it was more of a white lie. And the alternative meant losing the contract. Losing everything she had worked for.

"If I go with you—" she said it quickly, before she could change her mind "—I want a contract for the *castello* up front."

Leo felt triumph course through him as he felt Dara's shift toward accepting his offer. He'd seen the uncertainty on her face, knew the difficult position he was placing her in.

"You don't trust me, Dara?"

"Not even a little bit."

Don't miss
RESISTING THE SICILIAN PLAYBOY
by Amanda Cinelli,
available October 2015 wherever
Harlequin Presents® books and ebooks are sold.

www.Harlequin.com

HARLEQUIN
Presents®

Suave, sensual and utterly scandalous...

Leo Valente is as notorious as the tabloids say he is. But feisty wedding planner Dara Devlin isn't deterred. She needs his family castle for her top client, so she boldly accepts Leo's outrageous challenge to be his fake girlfriend!

WINNER
SO YOU THINK YOU CAN WRITE

SAVE $1.00

on the purchase of RESISTING THE SICILIAN PLAYBOY by Amanda Cinelli {available Sept. 15, 2015} or any other Harlequin Presents book.

Redeemable at participating outlets in the U.S. and Canada only. Not redeemable at Barnes and Noble stores. Limit one coupon per customer.

52612754

5 65373 00076 2   (8100)0 12069

COUPON EXPIRES OCT. 19, 2015

Available wherever books are sold, including most bookstores, supermarkets, drugstores and discount stores.

www.Harlequin.com